A Book of Magic Horses

A BOOK OF

MAGIC HORSES

Ruth Manning-Sanders

DRAWINGS BY
ROBIN JACQUES

METHUEN CHILDREN'S BOOKS

also by Ruth Manning-Sanders

A BOOK OF GIANTS

A BOOK OF DWARFS

A BOOK OF DRAGONS

A BOOK OF WITCHES

A BOOK OF WIZARDS

A BOOK OF MONSTERS

A BOOK OF GHOSTS AND GOBLINS

A BOOK OF DEVILS AND DEMONS

A BOOK OF CHARMS AND CHANGELINGS

A BOOK OF OGRES AND TROLLS

A BOOK OF SORCERERS AND SPELLS

A BOOK OF SPOOKS AND SPECTRES

A BOOK OF ENCHANTMENTS AND CURSES

A BOOK OF MAGIC ANIMALS

A BOOK OF CATS AND CREATURES

A BOOK OF KINGS AND QUEENS

A BOOK OF PRINCES AND PRINCESSES

A BOOK OF HEROES AND HEROINES

A BOOK OF MAGIC ADVENTURES

First published in Great Britain 1984
by Methuen Children's Books Ltd,
11 New Fetter Lane, London EC4P 4EE
Copyright © 1984 Ruth Manning-Sanders
Illustrations copyright © 1984 Robin Jacques
Reproduced, printed and bound in Great Britain by
Hazell Watson & Viney Limited,
Member of the BPCC Group,
Aylesbury, Bucks

British Library Cataloguing in Publication Data

Manning-Sanders, Ruth
  A book of magic horses.
  I. Title   II. Jacques, Robin
  823'.912[J]   PZ7

  ISBN 0-416-28070-6

Contents

For permission to retell Beedul-a-bup!
the author wishes to thank the Folklore Society.

1. *The Dapple Horse*

I

A farmer, who was a widower, had three sons. The sons grew up and the farmer grew old. He fell very ill and knew that he must die. So he called his sons to him and said, 'My lads, when I am dead, you must not quarrel. Each of you must take that which I leave you with my blessing. You, my eldest son, shall inherit the farm. You, my second son, shall have my flock of sheep; and you, my youngest, shall have the old dapple horse that stands in the stable and has done no work these many years.'

And after having so spoken the farmer died, and his three sons mourned greatly, for he had been good to them.

But life must be lived, one cannot mourn for ever. The eldest son took over the management of the farm, and that kept him busy enough. The second son took the flock of sheep, and drove them away to set up a farm of his own. The youngest son, whose name was Charlie, said to himself, 'And what am I to do? Stay here and be my brother's labourer? Nay, that will not do, lest my heart grow wild with jealousy. I must take my inheritance, the old horse, and ride away, though heaven knows where I am to go!'

Charlie went to the stable. There stood the dapple horse, so old, so lean, that his backbone stood out like the ridge of a roof.

Charlie looked at the old horse and muttered to himself, 'A useless thing! A useless thing!'

And you can imagine his surprise when the old horse began to speak. This is what he said: 'Boy, you are as stupid as a bean straw. No one should praise the day before the evening, and no one should lament either, before he knows what way the hare will run. Go to your brother and ask him to let you have the oldest saddle and the oldest bridle that hang in the harness-room.'

Well – to be ordered about by a horse! This was something one would never expect to happen. Charlie was so taken by surprise that he did just what the horse told him to do. He went to his brother and said, 'Brother I have come to take my leave of you. I and the old horse will ride away together. Give me, I pray you, the oldest saddle and the oldest bridle of all those that hang in the harness-room.'

'Why Charlie,' said his brother, 'what do you take me for? I am not so mean as all that! I had hoped that you would stay and work for me, and indeed I would have paid you well. But if you prefer to ride away and leave me, take the best saddle and bridle you can find.'

'I have orders to take the worst,' said Charlie.

'Orders?' said his brother in surprise. 'Whose orders?'

'The orders of the old dapple horse,' said Charlie.

'Poor lad,' thought Charlie's brother. 'Our father's death must have turned his brain.' But he told Charlie that of course he might take any saddle and bridle that suited him. And Charlie went away to the harness-room, snatched down from the wall the oldest saddle and bridle he could find, and carried them to the old horse in the stable.

The old horse looked at the saddle, looked at the bridle, and nodded his head approvingly. 'That's a good lad,' he said. 'Now on with the harness, and up on my back, and we'll be off.'

'Where to?' asked Charlie.

'To where I take you,' said the horse. 'And no more questions, if you please. This is no time for foolish prattling.'

'You are not exactly polite, are you?' said Charlie. But he did as the dapple horse told him. In a very short time he had the horse saddled and bridled, and was up on his back and riding away at a fast trot.

'I suppose you know where we are going,' said Charlie, 'but it's more than I do.'

'We are going to Dragon Island to rescue a princess and win you a beautiful bride,' said the horse.

'That sounds very pleasant,' said Charlie, 'but also very impossible.'

'Not at all impossible if you do as I tell you,' said the horse.

'Then I will do as you tell me,' answered Charlie.

So on they went and on; and at every step he took the horse was becoming younger and stronger looking. Now he was no longer old and skinny, but vigorous and young, with a proudly-arched neck and muscles that rippled under a coat that shone like satin.

'And if I am awake or if I am dreaming, I scarcely know,' said Charlie to himself, 'but I'm sure that I am past feeling surprised at anything that may happen.'

What did happen was that they arrived at the capital city of the country and entered the city and rode slowly along a street until they came into the square before the king's palace. Crowds of people were gathered in the square, and in front of the palace gates a town crier was ringing his bell and shouting, 'Oyez, Oyez, Oyez! The daughter of our lord the king has been stolen by a dragon and carried away across the sea. To the one who brings back his daughter the king will give her hand in marriage and also half the kingdom.'

'What are you waiting for now, boy?' said the horse. 'Off with you, into the palace and present yourself to the king. Because it is you who are going to bring back his daughter.'

'Oh goodness me, what next? It's really and truly too absurd!' said Charlie to himself. But all the same, and scarcely aware of what he was doing, there he was off the horse's back and striding in through the palace gates, and up to the great entrance door and knocking on the door, and being admitted by a lacquey and led into the presence of the king, and bowing low not once but many times, and straightening himself up again and saying, 'Your majesty, I have come to tell you that I will free your daughter and bring her back to you.'

The king was feeling sad enough, but he couldn't help giving a little smile. 'Well, my lad,' he said, 'you don't look to me just the right man to do such a thing as that. You are no knight, you have no armour, you are but scarce grown-up. But there, take my blessing. And here are three gold pieces to go with the blessing, because you will have to pay for your passage across the sea.'

Like one in a dream Charlie took the gold coins, and bowing again and again and walking backwards and feeling very awkward and silly, he went to join his horse in the courtyard. 'I suppose you know what you are doing, my horse,' he said, 'but I must admit that *I* don't!'

9

'What *you* have to do is to obey my orders,' said the horse. 'Mount, mount quickly, we have no time to lose!'

Now there was Charlie up on the horse's back again, and there was the horse off at a brisk trot, and never stopping until they came to the sea, where in a small sheltered bay an old fisherman was standing knee-deep in the water, dragging his boat ashore.

'Here's the fellow who will take us to Dragon Island,' said the horse, 'Speak to him, Charlie.'

'Good day, old friend,' said Charlie.

'Good day, young sir,' said the fisherman.

'And how has your fishing gone?' said Charlie feeling rather foolish

'Bad, very bad, as you can see by my empty net,' said the old man.

'Well,' said Charlie, 'I have a gold piece here, which I will give you if you will row me and my horse over to Dragon Island. And if I am lucky and you row myself and my horse and the princess back again, you shall have two more gold pieces.'

'You won't be lucky and you won't bring back the princess,' said the old man. 'For as sure as eggs is eggs the dragon will swallow you down, and swallow down that horse of yours as well. But I could do with that one gold piece, and so I'll row you over to the island, if you'll put that gold piece into my hand before you set foot on the island.'

'Right!' said Charlie. He helped the old man to push his boat out into deeper water, and then he and the horse and the old man got into the boat. Charlie took one oar, the old man took the other, the horse took the tiller, and there they were rowing away fast as fast on their way to Dragon Island.

And all the time the old man was staring at the horse and muttering, 'Holy Mother! What a creature! Got more sense in his head than many a human being!'

It was a long, long way to Dragon Island. In fact it took them nine whole days to reach it. And they might have starved had not the horse produced both food and drink, meat and bread and wine, and a bag of oats for himself from under the seat in the stern of the boat: a happening which made the old fisherman stare and wonder and mutter to himself, 'Marveel-ious! What a creature, what a creature!' But Charlie was beyond wondering at anything. To him it was all like a dream from which he had no wish to wake.

10

On the ninth morning they arrived before the island – an island of gigantically high cliffs with no harbour, not even one little bay or inlet. 'Well, now we're beaten,' said Charlie to himself. 'After coming all this way, it seems we have only to turn round and row home again.'

But the horse stood up in the boat and said, 'Put those fool thoughts out of your head. Up on my back and hold tight, because I'm going to jump.'

And scarcely had Charlie scrambled on to his back, when the horse did jump. With one mighty leap he was up at the top of the cliff. And there on a plateau at a little distance they could see the dragon's great castle. The castle was built of crystal, and so transparent that Charlie could see into all the rooms. And in one room he saw the young princess sitting in a silver chair with her head buried in her hands.

'Now, Charlie, in with you quickly, and bring out that poor young thing,' said the horse. 'But hurry, hurry! Because if the dragon should catch us, he will find us just handy for his evening meal!'

Charlie didn't need telling twice. He was off the horse's back in an instant, and racing across the plateau and in through the great door of the palace and up some silver-shining stairs and into the room where the princess sat, and panting out, 'I've come to fetch you home,' and taking her by the hand, and racing with her out of the palace over to where the horse was waiting, and lifting her on to the horse's back and getting up behind her. Now the horse was leaping down the cliff again. And there they were all three back safely in the boat.

'Eh,' said the old man, as he pushed off into deep water, 'there's stranger things happen in this world than a fellow would ever dream of. But if I'm three gold pieces the richer for 'em, I wouldn't mind if they happened again and again!'

II

So, not to weary you with too long a telling, it is enough to say that the boat got back to the mainland in safety. Charlie left the old fisherman well satisfied with the three gold pieces; and, with the princess up before him on the horse, made all speed back to the king's city. You can just imagine the welcome they got: flags waving, people singing and dancing in the streets, the king shedding tears of joy, flinging his arms round the princess, kissing her again and again; and then with the tears streaming down his cheeks, grasping Charlie by both hands, and telling him what a splendid fellow he was, and how he could never thank him enough, and that of course he should marry the princess, and that he would arrange for a magnificent wedding without delay.

Charlie felt quite bewildered by it all, but he also felt very, very happy, and he hurried to the royal stables where the horse was contentedly munching a good feed of oats. 'Oh, I am so happy, so happy, my horse,' he said. 'I am going to marry the princess – think of that! I, the humble son of a farmer, will become a prince – and I owe it all to you!'

The horse chewed his mouthful of oats, swallowed and said, 'It is not wise to hurrah before one is out of the wood. Have I proved right in all I have told you to do so far?'

'You have indeed, my horse.'

'Then obey me yet once again,' said the horse. 'When you go to the church to marry your bride, ride me, and *take the princess up before you on my back.*'

Charlie laughed. 'That doesn't sound a very dignified way of going to be wedded,' he said.

'Nevertheless, it is the right way,' said the horse. 'In fact it is the only safe way.'

'If the princess is willing – ' said Charlie.

The horse stamped angrily. 'Willing or no, I tell you. Willing or no!'

So came the wedding morning. The royal coach, all decorated with flowers and flags, was waiting to carry the king and the princess to church. Of course the king expected his daughter to ride beside him in the coach; but Charlie said no, the princess must ride on the horse with him. The king said that would be a very unusual way of proceeding, but the princess was delighted. 'Certainly I will ride on the darling horse,' she said. And of course she got her way.

And the royal procession set out for the church. First came the king's coach, then came the dapple horse with the princess, in her bridal robes and veil, perched before Charlie on the saddle. Then a long train of knights and squires and court ladies, some in carriages, some on horseback, watched by the crowd of townspeople who stood on either side of the way, waving flags and clapping hands and shouting 'Hurrah! Hurrah!'

'And isn't it a good omen,' said the princess to Charlie, 'that we have such a lovely sunny morning for our wedding!'

A good omen! But what was this? Suddenly the sky grew dark above them, and down out of a black cloud flew the dragon, eyes glaring, clawed hands waving, wide open mouth spitting fire. Down he darted upon the king's coach, flung it over, and then not finding the princess in it, turned with a howl of rage upon the dapple horse. The horse reared, the horse kicked, the princess screamed as the dragon's claws clutched at her dress. In another moment he would have dragged her off the horse, but the horse again reared and kicked, Charlie drew his sword, *flick, flack,* off went one clawed hand, *flick, flack* off went the other clawed hand, now just one more thrust and with a yell that seemed to set the whole world echoing, off went the dragon's head.

'Not a very pretty spectacle for a wedding morning,' said the dapple horse. 'But if his majesty the king is not hurt, we may say that all's well that ends well.'

His majesty the king was not hurt, but so terribly frightened that he could only gasp and shudder. Charlie suggested that they should put off the wedding until his majesty felt better, but the king gasped out, 'No, no! Let us get it over, let us get it over, before some other terrible thing happens!'

But no other terrible thing did happen. There was some delay whilst the street was cleared of the dragon's head and body, and the royal coach, which was smashed to pieces, was hauled out of the way, and the crowds of frightened townsfolk, who were rushing about in every direction, were brought to order by a herald's repeated proclamations that now all was well.

And all *was* well, both then and thereafter. The princess and Charlie were married. The king soon recovered from his fright, and he was loud in his praises of the dapple horse. 'That horse is worth more than all my army put together,' the king said. 'He has saved my daughter's life, and

13

truly I think he has saved mine. And though I personally cannot understand his language, it seems that he has the power of speech.

'He shall have a stable built of gold and a manger made of gold. He shall go in and out as he pleases, and work or be idle as he pleases. And every year on this date my people shall hold a holiday. There shall be music and dancing and free feasting for everybody. And the day shall be called not Sunday, nor Monday, nor Tuesday, nor Wednesday, nor Thursday, nor Friday, nor Saturday, but THE DAY OF THE DAPPLE HORSE.'

2. *Rubizal's Black Horse*

The great magician, Rubizal, lived in the mountains. Nobody knew quite what to make of him. Some people believed him to be an angel in disguise, because he would often help poor folk in trouble. Others believed him to be Satan's own brother, because he played such scurvy tricks on people he disliked. But everyone agreed that there was no other being at all like him. He was just Rubizal, and it was best to keep out of his way if you could, and never, never to speak ill of him.

But to keep out of Rubizal's way was not easy, because he could change himself into any shape he pleased: he might meet you in the guise of an old woman, or of a nobleman, of a fine horse, or even of a puppy or a rabbit.

And so, having told you all I know about Rubizal, I will tell you about the pedlar.

The pedlar had been to town, and was returning home across the mountains with a basket full of glassware – drinking cups and decanters, lampshades, flower vases, pretty little hand-mirrors and the like: goods which he hoped to sell to the farmer-folk and villagers in his own neighbourhood. The basket was heavy, and having toiled up a steep mountain path, the pedlar was tired and out of breath. So he sat down to rest on a big flat stone, put the basket by his side, and amused himself by reckoning up the profit he would make by the re-selling of the basket's contents.

'Fifteen pounds . . .' muttered the pedlar, 'or say eighteen . . . and then there's another ten . . . or maybe twelve for the mirrors – that makes forty pounds . . . and I ought to get another fifty or more on the lampshades and vases . . . Good! Pretty near a hundred pounds!'

Now all unseen by the pedlar, Rubizal had followed him up the hill, and at that moment was standing behind the pedlar's back, listening to his muttered words.

15

'Ho, ho!' thinks Rubizal, and 'Ha! ha!' thinks he. 'Here's a greedy fellow! There's too much profit-making going on in this chap's noddle!'

So what does Rubizal do, but take hold of the basket and turn it upside down.

Crash! There's all the precious glassware tumbled out of the basket and lying in shimmering bits and pieces at the pedlar's feet!

Oh me ! Oh me! Here's our pedlar wailing and lamenting. 'Now I've upset the basket! Now I am ruined! I have spent my last penny on all this glassware and now I have nothing! *Nothing!* Oh my poor wife, she will starve, and I shall starve. I can't go home with this sad news – oh, oh, I would rather cut my throat, if only I had a knife or a razor that would do the job. Oh, oh, there's nothing for it but to fling myself over a precipice and make an end!'

And he jumped off the stone, and stood looking wildly about him.

'You are in trouble, my friend?'

The pedlar turned round. What did he see? A rider on a beautiful black horse, a rider who had apparently just come up the mountain path. But that rider was no other than Rubizal; and Rubizal was now feeling just a little sorry for the mischief he had done.

'Trouble!' cried the pedlar. *'Trouble!* Look at this broken glass! All my savings gone in this smash! I am penniless, I say, penniless! How can I go home and tell my wife that I haven't even a penny for her to buy a loaf of bread? Out of my way – there is nothing before me but death!'

And he made a rush to get past the rider on the black horse.

But the rider leaned from the saddle and caught him by the arm. 'Nay, nay, my friend, that's not the way. I think your wife would rather see you whole, even if penniless, than find you lying at the bottom of some precipice, all in bits and pieces like your glassware. I would willingly help you, only I, alas, am also penniless. But I have an idea. Down in the next valley is an inn. Ah, the innkeeper is a mean and greedy fellow! He overcharges for every glass of beer his customers drink. He gets rich at other folk's expense. Now we will go visit him. We will play a fine trick on him, and he shall pay you for your broken glassware. Ah, this will be rare fun! Come!'

The pedlar took up his empty basket, and went with the rider down into the next valley. Now and then, where the way was very steep and

17

dangerous, the pedlar put up his hand to the horse's bridle and led it. He was feeling dazed and bewildered.

'But how can the innkeeper, if as you say he is greedy and grasping, be generous enough to give me money for my broken glass?' he asked.

'Generous!' laughed the rider. 'Nay, my friend, the innkeeper doesn't know the meaning of that word! Nevertheless, he will give you money. We are going to sell him my black horse.'

'Yes . . . but . . . my dear sir . . .' stammered the pedlar, 'I cannot take the money you get for the sale of your horse!'

'Pooh!' said the disguised Rubizal. 'I have other horses. And I have my own reasons for wishing to help you.'

(Indeed he had, the mischievous fellow, since it was he who had caused the breaking of the pedlar's glassware. But of this, the pedlar knew nothing.)

Well, they made their way down into the valley, and came to the inn. And there was the innkeeper standing at the door — an unpleasant-looking fellow, bursting with fat. Rubizal dismounted and the innkeeper eyed the black horse with approval.

'That's a handsome animal you have there,' he said. 'Never seen a better! I have some horses of my own, but this one beats them all hollow.'

'Worth his weight in gold,' said Rubizal. 'Never tires, and sweet-tempered too. If you will stable him, master innkeeper, I and my comrade will step into your parlour and refresh ourselves.'

The innkeeper called his boy. The boy led the black horse into the stable. And Rubizal and the pedlar went into the inn, where the innkeeper set meat and bread and ale on the table before them.

And whilst they ate, Rubizal told the innkeeper of the pedlar's misfortune, which made the innkeeper hold his fat sides and roar with laughter. That made the pedlar very angry; but Rubizal gave him a nudge and whispered, 'Hush! Leave me to manage this.'

The innkeeper laughed so loud that the black horse heard him and began to whinny.

'Ha!' said the innkeeper, mopping his eyes. 'Seems that animal wants to join in the fun! And how old is he?'

'Rising four.'

'What will you sell him for?' asked the innkeeper.

18

'He is not for sale.'

'A pity,' said the innkeeper. 'I could do with him. I lost just such another animal myself last week. Died on me.'

'You perhaps overfed it?' said Rubizal.

'Oh no, no, quite the contrary,' laughed the innkeeper. '*I'm* not one to pamper any beast!'

'Then I should be afraid to trust my animal to you,' said Rubizal. 'He is accustomed to live well.'

'And so he shall if you sell him to me,' said the innkeeper. 'All I meant was that my horse refused to eat, and died of it – not *my* fault. See now, I'll give you fifty pounds for your beast.'

'Nothing doing,' said Rubizal.

'Sixty pounds then?'

'Nothing doing.'

'Seventy pounds, eighty, ninety, a hundred – '

Rubizal kept shaking his head and saying no. But the more often he said no, the more eager the innkeeper became. Now he was jingling money in his pockets. Now he was throwing coins on to the table. And when he had put down five hundred pounds, Rubizal laughed, and said, 'It's a deal.'

The innkeeper hurried off to the stable to look at his new purchase. Rubizal gathered up the coins from the table, put them in a leather bag, and handed the bag to the pedlar.

'There, my friend,' he said, 'take that home to your good wife.'

The pedlar, quite overwhelmed by such generosity, began to stammer out his thanks. But Rubizal said, 'Nay, nay, my friend, you mustn't thank me. I owe you the money for the trick I played on you. For it was I, and none other, who tumbled your basket upside down and smashed your glassware. Now goodbye. If the innkeeper asks for me, tell him I have gone over the mountain. And so, God keep you!'

Woosh! In a puff of smoke, Rubizal vanished. And the pedlar, in a daze of bewilderment and joy, took up his basket and went out across the courtyard to the stable, where the innkeeper, who had already arranged a bedding of straw with his own hands for the black horse, was now bringing in a bundle of hay to put in the rack.

But what was the astonishment of the pedlar, and the terror of the innkeeper when the black horse, turning his head and giving the innkeeper a scornful look, *said* (Yes, *said* I tell you!) 'My good fellow, hay I do not eat, water I do not drink. Pray bring me some roast beef and toast, and a glass of wine.'

The innkeeper gave a shriek and ran out of the stable, bumping into the pedlar who stood open-mouthed at the stable door.

'Where is that Devil who sold me this hell-hound of an animal?' yelled the innkeeper.

'He has gone over the mountain,' said the pedlar.

'I'll give him over the mountain!' shouted the innkeeper. 'I'll have him up before the justice, I'll – I'll – '

The innkeeper's shouts had brought his neighbours running to see what was the matter. They came crowding into the stable. What did they see? No horse, whether of hell or heaven. No animal of any kind – only a little bunch of twigs hanging in a halter from the manger.

And the pedlar, thinking it was high time to make himself scarce, took up his empty basket and went home, to show his wife the leather bag full of money, and to tell her of his strange adventure.

3. Beedul-a-bup!

'Now I'll tell you a story,' said old Sam. 'It's about a princess called Suzanna, and the Devil, and his green Cock, and his three-legged horse, Tigerlily.

'Once upon a time there was a king who lived on an island. This king had a daughter, Suzanna, and that gal was a pet of her father's.

'One day a prince comes to ask for her in marriage.

'The father loves the young man, but the gal says, "Poppa, me don't like him." So the king her father promises Suzanna that any man she sees and likes he will agree to her marrying that one.

'One night a good friend of the king made a dance and invited Princess Suzanna to the ball.

'This man who made the dance invited all classes of people. So he invites Devil too, but they don't know that it's Devil.

'When all the guests come, everybody gives their name. Devil gives his name – Mister Winkler. So the ball begins.

'Devil saw the gal. He went and asked her if she wished to dance with him.

'The gal was so glad she said, "Yes, sir, for I love you the most."

'They dance till daylight, but the gal don't want to leave Devil.

'She says to Devil, "Come, have a walk home with me."

'Devil says, "Yes, I would go, but I am a man have such a great business, I has to go home very soon to seek after it."

'The gal says, "Come, go home with me and you will get me to marry, for my father is a king."

'And as Devil hears about marrying he goes home with the gal.

'When she gets to the house she calls to her father, "Poppa, here comes my lover, I have found him at last."

21

'The servant-boy who knew a thing or two, said, "Young mistress, that man is Devil."

'The gal gets vexed, she begins to cry.

'She goes to her father crying, and tells him "The servant-boy abused me most shameful."

'The father gets angry, comes out to the boy, doesn't ask the boy anything but puts him in prison.

'They take Mister Winkler into the palace, and the father fixes everything up and they get married.

'After Mister Winkler got married he said, "I am ready to go."

'The king says, "No, I can't send away my one daughter. You must stay and I will make you a king too."

'Mister Winkler says "No."

'During this time they don't know that it's Devil, that's why when the boy told them they got angry.

'Devil has married ten times and eaten all his wives. Now he was going to eat this princess too.

'So, as he's anxious to go, the gal has to go with him.

'When they are ready to start, the father gives them a long bag full of money. Devil gets a boatman, and they set off across the sea.

'They sail four days before they get to their home.

'When the gal got there, she met an old lady in the house. This lady was Devil's cook.

'As Devil got in he said to the cook, "I have got a good fat meat for the party."

'So Devil goes and locks the gal into a barred-up room, and leaves the old lady to watch if the gal is going to get away. He leaves a green Cock that any time the old lady says that the gal is getting away the Cock must call, and he leaves a bag of corn to feed the Cock that he may keep good watch.

'The old lady says "Yes."

'Devil orders his three-legged horse, Tigerlily, to be saddled, because he is going to invite his friend to come and help him eat the gal.

'Devil rides off.

'Devil's horse Tigerlily with his three legs goes galloping, galloping, *Beedul-a-bup! Beedul-a-bup!*

'When Devil gets about a mile away the old lady goes in to the gal, takes her out and tells her, "Your husband is Devil, and he is going to eat you."

'The gal begins to cry.

'The old lady says, "Don't cry, I love you and I am going to let you go, but the green Cock is a watchman, and if he sees you getting away he will call for his master. But never mind I will try what I can do."

'The old lady gets ten quarts of corn and a gallon of rum, soaks the corn in the rum for about an hour, and then she gives it to the green Cock.

'The green Cock eats the whole evening till night, and after he's finished eating, he drops asleep.

'Then the old lady gets a boatman and pays him. And the boatman takes the gal over the sea.

'When it's nearly daylight, the green Cock wakes and goes to look through a hole in the door if he can see the gal. But the gal is gone. So Cock goes to the cook and asks.

'The cook says, "She's gone. I was calling you but you didn't wake."

23

'Then the green Cock sings out:

"Mister Winkler, Winkler oh!
Coo-coo-ree-co!
The gal is gone!
Awake me wake,
Go look through hole,
The gal was gone!"

'Horse Tigerlily hears, and says, "Master turn back! Master turn back! Cock is calling. The gal is gone!"

'Then Mister Winkler turns back and is coming like lightning on Tigerlily, his three-legged horse, *Beedul-a-bup! Beedul-a-bup!*

'Mr Winkler calls out "Me coming!" *Beedul-a-bup!* "Me coming!" *Beedul-a-bup! Beedul-a-bup! Beedul-a-bup!*

'At last he reaches the yard and sees the gal is gone. He gets a canoe and starts after her, and by next daylight he sees gal's boat but far away.

'He calls out:

"Suzanna dear upon the sea,
Suzanna dear upon the sea,
Come back my darling, back to me!
Your husband here is calling thee!"

'When the gal looks back she says, "Shove ahead, boatman, do, to save my life!"

And by the time they got to land Devil was near them.

'And the boatman shot off a piece of Devil's canoe and water got in, so Devil had to go back home.

'And believe it or not, following the gal's boat, horse Tigerlily came swimming and calling out, "Me coming too! Me coming too! Don't want to be Devil's horse! Want to be gal's horse! Want to live with princess!" And come he did and followed the princess to the king's court.

'When the gal gets back home she tells her father about Devil, and the father says, "You see, you silly gal, you should have married the prince."

'And the gal says, "Poppa, I will marry the prince."

'So they held the wedding, and I was there. They let the servant boy out of prison and he was there too. We were feasting and dancing; and horse Tigerlily was feasting and dancing — *Beedul-a-bup, bup-bup, beedul-a-bup, bup-bup!* — with the best of us. We danced till the clock struck twelve. And then we all went to bed.

'And horse Tigerlily lived with the princess ever after.'

4. The Adventures of Gregor

The Fisherman and the Devil

Once upon a time there was a king who, though not exactly greedy, thought a great deal about what he ate and drank. And this king went on his travels into a neighbouring country, and was served at a banquet with some fish that he had never before tasted.

'My good fellow,' said the king to his host, 'this fish is really delicious. May I ask its name?'

'Oh that is a moranian,' said his host. 'I am flattered that it so pleases you. Moranians are abundant in our waters.'

'Well,' said the king, 'if moranians are abundant in your waters, they should also be abundant in mine, seeing that our countries have both the same coastline.'

Now you must know that the king employed a fisherman, called Casimer, whose duty it was to provide fish every day for the royal household. And when the king returned to his own country he sent for Casimer and said to him, 'How is it that among all the fish that you send up daily to the palace, you have never yet provided me with moranians?'

'Moranians, your majesty?' said Casimer. 'I never heard tell of them. There are no such fish in our waters.'

'Rubbish!' snapped the king. 'If you think you can get away with that tale, you are mistaken. I suspect that you and your wife have such a liking for the fish that you keep them all for your own table. But that won't do, my man! See that within three days you send up to the palace a goodly supply of this fish, or – well, you can pack up and be off, for I shall employ another fisherman.'

26

Casimer bowed low, and went back to the little house where he lived with his wife. He felt utterly miserable. But he tried to be cheerful, and he said nothing about his trouble to his wife, because she was going to have a baby very soon, and he didn't want to distress her.

'Why did the king send for you?' asked his wife anxiously.

'Oh just to tell me to send up all the fish I could catch,' said Casimer. 'I suppose he's entertaining company.'

And he took his net, went down to the shore, got into his boat, pushed off into the sea, and cast his net into the water.

That day he pulled in his net heavy with fish. He caught cod, herring, mackerel, and many another kind of fish, but no fish that he was unacquainted with, no fish that could possibly be a moranian. He cast in his net again and again, he caught fish without number, but, alas, nothing new, and certainly no moranian.

He went home at last, heavy of heart, but determined to smile, so that he might not upset his wife.

Outside his house a little maiden from the king's court was waiting for him.

'Oh, oh, Casimer,' cried the little maiden, '*such* news! Your wife has given birth to a son, and almost at the same moment the queen gave birth to a daughter. The king said it was a good omen, and he sent down a litter to bring your wife and baby to the palace. Your wife is to be nurse to both the babies, and the king says he will keep your little son to be a playmate for his little daughter. Only think of it, Casimer, *your* baby to be the adopted brother of a princess! My word, I think your fortune is made!'

Well, that certainly was an astonishing piece of news! But it didn't make Casimer feel particularly happy. He would rather have kept his little son to himself, and — oh me! Now it seemed he was to lose both his son and his living, because he had not been able to catch that wretched fish — the moranian!

But there was nothing for it but to try again. He sat down to a lonely supper, went to a lonely bed, got up to a lonely breakfast, and having eaten, went down to the sea once more.

There was a stranger walking up and down on the beach — a tall, imposing-looking man, wearing a short jacket, thigh boots, and an enormous sou'-wester on his head. He didn't look like a sailor, he didn't look like a fisherman, he didn't look exactly like a gentleman, or a merchant, or a tradesman, or any kind of man Casimer had ever met with in all his life. And his voice when he greeted Casimer, sounded louder and clearer than the voice of the sea itself.

'Good day to you, fisherman!'

'Good day to you, sir.'

'You seem down in the dumps, fisherman!'

'And why shouldn't I be?' said Casimer. 'There is nothing to make merry about that I can see. The king has ordered me to catch him moranian, a fish I have never seen nor heard of. If I don't supply him with this wretched fish I am to lose my job; and to add to all, the king has carried my wife and my new-born son off to the palace. Am I to lose wife, son, and job all at one blow? It's enough to drive a fellow crazy!'

'Oh come, come,' said the stranger, 'you need not despair. In my youth I studied magic, and I am able to help you. If you will give me your son to serve me, when he is fifteen years old, I will fill the sea with moranians for you, in greater numbers than you can catch. And I assure you, fisherman, that I am a good master,' said the stranger with a gracious smile. 'I will treat your son with all the kindness he deserves.'

Casimer hesitated. To hand over his son to the stranger would be getting his own back on the king! And if he himself was not to have his son — well, why not this handsome stranger?

'Oh, all right,' he said grumpily.

The stranger took a piece of parchment from his pocket, and a pen from behind his ear. He wrote some words on the parchment, and handed the parchment to Casimer. 'Sign here, if you please,' he said, pointing with his pen to the bottom of the parchment.

'I must first know what I'm signing,' said Casimer. 'I'm not much of a hand at reading.'

'Just to say that you will allow your son to enter my service when he is fifteen years old,' said the stranger.

'Oh, all right,' said Casimer again.

But Casimer didn't much like it when the stranger pushed the nib of the pen into Casimer's finger and made it bleed, so that when Casimer signed his name it was written in his own blood.

'Good!' said the stranger, tucking the parchment back in his pocket. 'Now run out your boat, drop your net, and see what you will catch.'

Then with a farewell wave of his hand, the stranger vanished.

And Casimer ran his boat out into the sea, and cast his net into the water.

Yes, as the stranger had promised, the sea was swarming with that strange fish, the moranian. Casimer pulled in netfull after netfull, until his boat was piled high with them. And when the boat could hold no more, Casimer rowed back to shore, made fast his boat to a shore line, and went up to the palace to ask the king for a pony and cart.

'Seeing as I've caught more moranians than I can possibly carry,' he said. 'But I've paid dearly enough for those accursed fish,' he added.

And he told the king about the stranger, and about the paper he had signed.

The king was horrified. 'Oh, Casimer, what have you done?' he cried. 'Have you served me all these years, and not realized what a hasty temper I have? You ought to have known that I didn't mean a word of what I said, no, not one word! How could I have dismissed you from my service for the sake of a few moranians? I will never eat one of those devilish fish if I live to be a hundred. I would starve rather! Fling them back into the sea, Casimer! As for your little son, he shall stay here with me in the palace. I will bring him up as my own son, yes, as a royal prince. And surely not even the Devil himself will have the impudence to claim the service of a prince!'

'You may do as you please,' said Casimer sulkily. 'I am an unhappy man from this day forth.'

And he went back to his lonely little house, with not even his wife to share his sorrow. Though of course, as soon as the babies were weaned, his wife came home to him.

Meantime the king held a grand christening feast. His baby daughter was christened Ursula Susanka Gabriella Sophia; and Casimer's little son was christened Gregor Sebastian Sigismund — a name that was affection-ately shortened by the king and queen into Greg.

Little Greg knew no other than that the king was his father, the queen his mother, and princess Ursula his sister. The children were very fond of one another, they played together, they rode out together on two tiny ponies; by and by they did their lessons together. They loved each other dearly.

29

As soon as Gregor was old enough the king had him trained in all knightly skills; he even allowed him to drill the soldiers. He decided that when Gregor grew up he would make him his heir, and give him in marriage to Ursula. 'But in the meantime we will let him believe that Ursula is his sister,' the king said to the queen.

'Yes, that is best,' said the queen. 'But oh, sometimes I am filled with terror. When he is fifteen years old – '

'We needn't think of that!' said the king hastily.

But the king did think of it, and so did the queen. And as the years passed they thought of it more and more. And when Gregor's fifteenth birthday grew near, the queen would often be weeping. And the king became sadder day by day.

'Father,' said Gregor one morning, 'is anything the matter?'

'No, my boy, no,' said the king. 'How should there be?'

'But you look so unhappy, Father,' said Gregor. 'And Mother is always crying. Have I done anything to vex you?'

'Oh no, no,' said the king, 'you never vex me!'

'Then *what* is it?' said Gregor.

'Well,' said the king, trying to laugh, 'I suppose the queen and I are growing old. You can't expect old folk to laugh and make merry after the fashion of young folk.'

'No, it is not that!' cried Gregor. 'It is not that! I think you have some secret sorrow. And I beg you, I pray you to tell me what it is, that I may try to ease it. I am only a boy, but – but if you have enemies I will march at the head of your armies to fight them. If you are in need of a magic herb to heal some secret sickness, I will ride out and seek for it. If you are troubled because sister Ursula has as yet no suitors, I will have her portrait painted and travel from land to land, showing her portrait to kings and emperors and everywhere proclaiming her beauty and her goodness . . . Though perhaps I am still a little young for that,' he added thoughtfully. 'But oh, there is one thing I cannot bear – and that is to see you so unhappy, my father!'

So Gregor bothered and bothered, until at last the king could stand it no longer, and bursting into tears, told the boy the whole story: all about his real father, Casimer, and about the moranians, and how he, the king, had insisted on having such fish caught for him, and how fisherman

Casimer, in order to obtain those fish, had made a compact with the Devil.

'And the price Casimer paid for those wretched fish is your dear, dear self, Greg, to be given to the Devil when you are fifteen years' old.'

'But *I* signed no such compact,' said Gregor. 'I am not bound by it! Take heart, my dear lord king, whom I may no longer call Father. Let Satan do his worst, I do not fear him!'

And he left the king and went to call upon a priest, who was a friend of his. To this priest he told the whole story: and the priest gave him some good advice, and also a little book.

'This is a holy book,' said the priest. 'Put it into your pocket, my lad, and keep it carefully. I don't promise that it will save you, but I hope it may. You are a good lad, and though evil is mighty, good is mightier.'

II   The Hut in the Desert

So on the morning of his fifteenth birthday, Gregor rose before dawn, and tiptoeing out of the palace that he might wake no one, greeted the guard who stood at the palace gate with a hearty 'good morning', hastened down to the beach where his father Casimer kept his boat, found the boat drawn up on the sand, and stood beside it and waited.

He hadn't long to wait. In a whirl of wind that nearly flung Gregor off his feet, came Satan, snatched up Gregor in his clawlike hands, and soared with him high, high into the air.

For hundreds of miles Satan flew on and on under the blue vault of the sky, and then he gave a sudden yell and shouted, 'You have something with you, and that you must throw away.'

'I throw nothing away,' said Gregor. 'I keep what is mine.'

Satan flew on, he flew for two hundred miles. Then he yelled again, 'Do you see the waves of ocean beneath us?'

'No,' said Gregor, 'you clasp me so tightly that I see nothing but your ugly self.'

'Cast what you are holding into the ocean,' screamed Satan. 'Or I will cast *you* down!'

'That would be a pleasant change for me,' said Gregor. 'I am quite a good swimmer.'

Satan gave another, louder yell. He flew on and on. Over the waves he flew, and having crossed the ocean, he swooped low and landed in a sandy desert. And there he set Gregor down.

'I must rest, I must rest,' panted Satan. 'The weight of that book of yours is heavier than all the mountains in the world. If you don't throw it away, I will set fire to both you and it!'

'I see no reason why you shouldn't rest, you poor old fellow,' said Gregor. 'But why you have taken the trouble to fly so fast and so far is more than I can guess.'

Now Gregor had a little dagger in his belt, and whilst Satan sat and panted, Gregor took the dagger from its sheath and swiftly drew a circle in the sand round Satan and himself.

'What are you up to now?' panted Satan.

'Oh, just amusing myself,' said Gregor.

And within the circle he drew a cross.

When Satan saw that cross he screamed. 'Tread out that cursed sign, tread it out, I say!'

'Nay,' said Gregor, 'I will leave you to do that for yourself.'

And he stepped out of the circle, and made to go on his way.

Now Satan was in a panic. He feared he might have to sit there in the wilderness until judgement day. For the sign of the cross took away all his strength so that he couldn't step out of the circle.

'Boy, boy,' he yelled, 'is this fair dealing? I bought you from your father in all honesty, I gave him in exchange for you just what he asked for. I did not cheat him, and yet you would cheat me!'

'Well,' answered Gregor, 'there's something in what you say. I will let you out of the circle if you will give me back the paper my father signed. Then we can both start fair again. You can go your way, and I will go mine.'

'No, I won't give it you back!' shrieked Satan.

'Then I will bid you good morning,' said Gregor.

And he turned to go.

'Stop, stop!' screamed Satan. 'I will give you gold, I will give you jewels, I will make you the richest man that ever lived!'

'I don't see that riches would do me much good in *your* kingdom,' laughed Gregor. 'It is not riches I would have from you.'

'Then what, *what?*' screamed Satan.

'Just the paper you forced my father to sign,' said Gregor. 'Give me that paper and I will open the circle.'

'No, no,' screamed Satan, 'you shall *not* have it!'

'Then good day to you,' said Gregor.

And he walked off.

But he hadn't gone more than a few paces when Satan was screaming after him again. 'You shall have it! You shall have it! You shall have the accursed paper!'

Gregor turned back then. He held out his hand. Satan took the signed paper from behind his ear, where he had kept it safely for fifteen years. Glaring, gnashing his teeth with impotent rage, he put the paper into Gregor's hand. And Gregor tore it across and across; he tore it into tiny fragments and scattered the fragments over the desert sand. Then with his foot he wiped out the sign of the cross within the circle, and began in a leisurely fashion to tread out the circle itself. But Satan had already leaped up into the air. And up he went, and up.

Gregor stood and watched him growing smaller and smaller, until he disappeared among the clouds.

'So much for you, and a good riddance,' said Gregor. 'Now that you are gone, I don't mind admitting that you thoroughly scared me!'

And he walked on.

But where was Gregor going? He couldn't tell. All around him, before and behind, as far as eye could see, nothing but desert sand, not a tree, not a bush. He was hungry and thirsty, but there was nothing that he could eat, and nothing wherewith to quench his thirst.

'I can but walk on,' he said to himself. 'And if I drop — why then I drop. It's better, I suppose, to die on earth than to live in Hell . . . But oh, come, come, courage, my lad! Lift up your heart — you're not dead yet!'

All through that day Gregor was walking on. He walked until his limbs ached and his feet staggered, and still there was nothing to see before him or behind him, but the desert sands. Now the sun set, now it was twilight, now it was night, and still he was staggering on . . . And then suddenly, not far ahead of him, there glowed a little light.

A light, a light! Surely then some living being beside himself in this terrible solitude! With all the strength that remained in him Gregor ran towards that light – and fell unconscious at the door of a little hut.

When he came to himself, he was slouched in an armchair before a bright fire in a small kitchen, and an old man was bending over him, holding a cup of wine to his lips.

'Good,' said the old man. 'You'll do now. Come drink this down.'

Gregor drank, sat up, smiled. 'Thank you,' he said, 'perhaps I – I ought to explain. I don't want to be a nuisance.'

'You will explain nothing tonight,' said the old man. 'I have a little room here behind the kitchen, where I keep a bed made up for such travellers as you. Though I must say,' he added with a chuckle, 'such travellers are few and far between. In fact I cannot recollect that any traveller has come this way during the past two hundred years.'

And if that was a strange remark, Gregor didn't notice it for he was soon in bed and fast asleep. Next morning he woke feeling as fit and well as he had ever felt in his life.

And there was the old man standing at the bedside and smiling.

'A pump in the yard behind the hut,' said the old man. 'Your clothes here on the chair, and breakfast waiting in the kitchen. Don't hurry yourself unduly, but don't be longer than you can help.'

So Gregor washed and dressed and sat down to breakfast with the old man. He wanted to tell the old man all about everything that had happened to him. But the old man said, 'Oh, never mind, never mind, that's ancient history. Now, Gregor, you are going to live with me. And we mustn't neglect your education. A lad of fifteen has yet much to learn.'

'You – you know my name?' said Gregor.

'In the course of a long life one comes to know many things,' said the old man with a chuckle.

So for three years Gregor lived there in the desert with the old man. And far from being treated as the prince whom Gregor had for so long believed himself to be, he now found that he was expected to make himself useful. He must dust, sweep, and clean like any lacquey, and he must be quick about his work too; for when he had finished it, there was the old man waiting to set him sums, to have him read history, to converse with him in many languages, and to read with him from the holy book which had so weighed down the devil.

The old man was a stern master. 'You must learn, you must learn, Gregor,' he said. 'If there's one thing I cannot stand, it's ignorance. I forbid you, do you hear, I absolutely forbid you, to waste your time.'

And Gregor, remembering how the old man had probably saved his life, was grateful, and did his best to please him.

When his tasks were done, the old man would send Gregor out 'to take the air' as he said. And about this 'taking of the air' there was something that Gregor must do, and something that he must not do. Outside the hut there were two roads, one going round the hut to the right, the other going round the hut to the left. 'You must always take the road to the left,' the old man told him. 'Never, never take the road to the right. Do you hear, and will you obey me?'

'Yes, master,' said Gregor, 'I hear, and I will obey.'

But to be always taking the same road became very monotonous, especially as that road was stony and full of potholes, and led nowhere but to more desert, more sand, with neither bush nor tree nor sound of singing bird. The road to the right, on the other hand, looked invitingly broad and firm: and surely, surely, there came wafting from it the scent of flowers, and a little whispering rustle as of a gentle wind murmuring to itself among leafy tree branches. It was altogether too inviting, and one day Gregor took just the shortest, shortest stroll along that forbidden way. The he remembered his master's words, and hurried back to the hut.

The old man was sitting in a rocking chair under the window. He seemed deep in thought. But he looked up and smiled when Gregor came in.

'Master,' said Gregor, 'I have done wrong. Today in my walk I went a little way – oh, only a little way – along the road to the right. Then my conscience smote me, and I turned back. But, oh master, there was a voice sounding in my ear, as if the road were calling me. A voice that was saying, "Come! *Come*!" '

The man sighed. 'If that is what the road said, I must not keep you here. Go, my lad, go. Go with my blessing.'

Gregor knelt to receive the old man's blessing. He kissed the old man's hand, he thanked the old man from his heart for all he had done for him. Then, with his dagger in his belt and the holy book in his pocket, Gregor went out of the hut and took the road to the right.

III   The White Horse

On and on went Gregor along that pleasant way. The birds sang; the trees rustled their branches; a little breeze, sweet with the scent of flowers, fanned his cheek. How delightful it was to have turned his back on the sands of that desert! How delightful it was to be young and strong, and to feel that he was at last setting out on his adventures like any legendary hero!

'This is life!' he said to himself. 'I have dawdled too long on the outskirts of it. Now I have put away childish things – now I am a man indeed!'

But Gregor, in his excitement, had overlooked one important matter. A man, be he never so heroic, must eat and drink. And by and by Gregor's stomach began to feel uncomfortably empty, and his throat uncomfortably dry. What was he to do? Turn back? Never! Surely if he walked on, this flowery road must, in the end, lead to some human habitation where he might crave food and drink. So on he went.

And now the road was twisting and turning like any snake: and then – oh see, on the right of the road a grassy hollow with a stream prattling merrily through it, and beside the stream an apple tree laden with fruit; and under the apple tree lay a white horse, sound asleep.

Now Gregor was stooping over the stream, cupping the water in his hands, drinking the water down in eager, grateful gulps. And now he was up the tree, picking the apples, setting his teeth into them, chewing and swallowing them down, no less gratefully.

He ate until his hunger was satisfied. And then he heard a voice speaking from under the tree.

'Had enough?' said the voice.

'Yes, thank you,' said Gregor. And then in sudden surprise: 'But who is speaking?'

'The white horse, at your service,' said the voice.

Yes, indeed it *was* the horse speaking. He was standing up now under the apple tree, and he was giving orders to Gregor in a most masterly fashion.

'Pick three more apples, put them in your pocket, and come down. Behind the tree you will find a saddle and bridle lying on a bush. Take them, harness me, and get on my back. It is I who am to carry you on the rest of your journey.'

Gregor did as the horse told him. He picked the three apples; he found the saddle and the bridle, he harnessed the horse, he leaped onto the horse's back, and the horse set off at a gallop.

'It is a wise lad that asks no questions,' said the horse, half turning his head over his shoulder. 'But doubtless you would like to know where we are going. Well, I will tell you. We are going to rescue your little playmate, the Princess Ursula. Not long after you left to keep your father's compact with Satan, the foolish little maiden missed you so sorely that she set out to look for you. And as she was wandering about, Satan met her. And thinking, I suppose, that since he had lost you, he would at least have her, he snatched her up and flew off with her. But knowing that she, in her innocence, was no fit denizen for Hell, he imprisoned her in a castle on an island in the midst of the sea. Now it is you and I who are going to her rescue; for we *can* rescue her, if you will be guided by me, and do everything that I tell you to do.'

'Oh yes, yes, I will do everything you tell me, my horse,' cried Gregor, 'for I feel it is all my fault!'

'No, not exactly your fault, Gregor,' said the horse. 'Say rather, your misfortune. It seems you were born to make trouble for those who love you . . . But here we are on the shore of the great ocean that surrounds the world. Now take one of those apples out of your pocket and cast it into the sea.'

Gregor did that, and there – did you ever? – the apple turned into a great golden road, stretching away and away along the surface of the sea, as far as eye could reach. And the white horse set off at a fast gallop along this road: and far off, at the end of the road, Gregor could see a dark hump, and something that gleamed faintly white on the top of the hump. And as they drew nearer, he saw that the dark hump was an island, and the faintly gleaming whiteness a high tower.

'It is in that tower that you will find the Princess Ursula,' panted the horse, whose sides were heaving from the speed of his gallop. 'We must hurry. In one short hour Satan will be coming to bully the princess. He visits her every day, just after the sun has gone down into the sea. But today we shall be before him. Now hold with hands, and grip with knees, for we must go faster yet.'

So with one last tremendous spurt, the horse came to the end of the road, and landed with a leap, that almost flung Gregor off his back, at the great entrance door of the tower.

'Now down with you, Gregor,' panted the horse. 'The tower door is locked but you have still two apples. Fling one of them at the door, and it will open. Go in, you will find the princess in a little room at the top of the tower. Don't linger to explain anything, but bring her down to me, swiftly, *swiftly*!'

Gregor slid down from the horse's back, and flung his second apple at the tower door. Immediately, the door swung open and Gregor rushed in, and up a winding stair, up and up, to a little bare room at the very top. And there he found the Princess Ursula, sitting forlornly on a three-legged stool and sobbing pitifully.

'Ursula! My dear, darling little Ursula!'

'Oh Greg, Greg!' Now the little princess was on her feet, she was flinging her arms round Gregor, she was hugging and kissing him. 'Oh Greg, I have been so frightened!'

'I have come to rescue you, my darling, but we must hurry.'

And hand in hand they ran down the winding stairs, and out through the open door of the tower, to where the white horse was waiting.

'Well done!' said the horse. 'Now up on my back the two of you – we haven't a moment to lose. Do you hear a far-off howling over there in the west, where the sun shoots up his last rays, before he bids the world goodnight, and sinks into the sea? That is the howling of Satan and his troop of lesser devils. This very night he plans to hold his hellish wedding

ceremony, and take your little princess for his bride. But I think we shall outwit him yet!'

And so saying the horse, with Gregor and Ursula on his back, set off at a furious gallop.

On what road was he galloping? That is indeed a mystery; for the golden road had ended when it reached the island. And now the landscape was becoming familiar to Gregor.

'I think we must be nearing your father's kingdom,' he said to Ursula. 'And surely there we shall be safe.'

'Safe!' The horse gave a snort of derision. 'Look behind you!'

Gregor glanced over his shoulder. Oh horror! Scarce a quarter of a mile behind them came Satan and all his troop, whirling along on fiery dragons, with hell hounds baying at the dragons' heels.

'Throw your last apple into the air,' panted the horse.

Hastily Gregor flung up that last apple. What happened? Up high above the earth rose the white horse and his riders. The white horse became the twilight sky, Gregor became the moon, and princess Ursula became the evening star . . . And down below them, Satan and all his troops galloped howling back to Hell.

Now there is little more for me to tell or for you to read. Of course when Satan had gone back to Hell, the white horse and Gregor and the princess came down from the sky, and continued their journey, and came safely home. Of course Gregor married the princess, and of course Gregor's father and mother were honoured by the king, and given a manor house and a goodly stretch of fertile ground, where Gregor's father, Casimer, might potter to his heart's content, or go fishing in the sea when the fancy so took him. But of that strange fish, the moranian, he never got another glimpse, nor did he wish to.

Ah, but there *is* something more to tell, and that something is very interesting. On the morning after the wedding, happy Gregor went to pay a visit to the white horse, whom he had left well-cared for in the king's stables. And what was his astonishment to find that the white horse was not there, but that someone else *was* there, and that was his former master, the old man with whom he had lived for those three years in the desert.

The old man was sitting on a heap of straw, reading in a big book.

40

'You are surprised to see me, Gregor, my lad,' chuckled the old man. 'And yet you have been seeing me day and night ever since you left my hut in the desert, and came to the grassy hollow and found the white horse asleep under the apple tree.

'I was that horse, Gregor. It was I who carried you safely through your travels. And a pretty mess you would have made of things without me! But now, having seen you safely home and happily married, I can go back to my desert with a tranquil heart. I do not think you will need me again; but if you do need me, you will find me with you. In the meantime, you have my blessing.'

And so having said, the old man waved his hand, and vanished.

5. Whoa-Ho!

A soldier served in the army in the city of Saratov. He was billeted in the house of an old woman who had a lovely daughter, already grown up. Of course the soldier fell in love with this daughter, and so he married her. The old woman died. The soldier lived with his wife, just the two of them. He carried out his military service but he lived at home. The soldier didn't know that his wife was a witch; it was lucky for him that she was a good witch and not a bad one.

Well now, one summer evening the soldier was lying down to rest after his supper. His wife tidied everything in the room and then she began to dress herself up. Half-awake the soldier watched her. 'Where can she be going?' he thought. She finished dressing up, she walked over to a shelf, she took a little bottle, and with something out of the bottle she anointed her nose.

What happened then? She turned into a magpie! The magpie flew up the chimney and away.

Then the soldier, greatly astonished, got up, went to the shelf, took the little bottle and anointed his own nose.

Then what happened? He turned into a magpie, he leapt up and out of the chimney and flew away.

He flew and flew and flew — my word, what a long flight for a magpie! He came to an island in the sea. There he alighted. No sooner did his feet touch the ground than he became a soldier again. He walked along the beach and suddenly he met his wife.

'And what are you doing here?' she asked.

'I don't know myself what I am doing here!' said the soldier.

'Go away quickly,' said his wife, 'before the other witches come flying, lest they eat you!'

'How can I go away when the sea is all round me?'

'Look now, I will give you a horse,' she said.

She drew on the sand with her finger the outline of a horse, and immediately there stood before her a raven-black stallion colt. She swung her husband up on to the back of the colt, and said, 'Don't try to stop the colt. Don't say "Whoa!" whatever you do, or it will be the worse for you!' The she gave the colt a slap and the colt rushed away. The soldier clung to the colt's neck. He looked down and saw the water below him, but the colt's feet were not touching the water. Over the sea they went at a furious gallop. When they reached the mainland the colt rose up higher and the tops of the forest trees came into sight under his galloping hooves.

The sun set. Now it was getting dark. Ahead of them shone the lights of a town.

'Aha!' thought the soldier. 'This must be my own town, Saratov!'

But the colt was rushing through the air past the town! Already the lights were fading away in the distance behind them!

'Stop, stop!' cried the soldier. *'Whoa! Whoa-ho-ho!'*

No sooner had the soldier spoken those words than the colt vanished from under him. The soldier fell to the ground, rolling over and over. Where was he now? In a deep dark forest. With great difficulty he got out of the forest and found his way to a high road.

It took him six months to walk home.

6. The Straw Horse

Once upon a time there lived an old man and an old woman. They were so poor! They had nothing. What they earned they ate up. And then again they had nothing.

One day the old woman said to the old man, 'Make a horse for me out of straw, old man, and smear it with tar.'

'What are you talking about?' said the old man. 'What can we do with a horse like that?'

'You just make it. I know very well what I shall do with it.'

So the old man made a straw horse and smeared it with tar.

They slept through the night. In the morning the old woman took her knitting and drove the Straw Horse out to graze. She sat by a little hillock. She knitted and sang:

> '*Graze, graze, little horse, in the sweet green grass,*
> *While I knit,*
> *Graze, graze, little horse, in the sweet green grass.*'

And as she sang and knitted, she fell asleep.

Then out of the dark wood, out of the great forest, came a Bear bustling along to the Straw Horse and said to him, 'Who and what are you? Speak up! Tell me!'

The Straw Horse said, 'I am a three-year-old horse, made of straw and smeared with tar.'

Then said the Bear, 'If you are made of straw and smeared with tar give me some of your tar to make me look as nice as you do.'

'Take some,' said the Straw Horse.

Then the Bear sank his teeth into the tar and tried to pull the tar off the Straw Horse. But his jaws stuck fast to the tar and he couldn't get away.

The Straw Horse walked off home dragging the Bear along with him.

When the old woman woke up the Straw Horse was nowhere in sight.

'Alas, old fool that I am' said she. 'Where is my Straw Horse then? Ah! Perhaps he has gone home.'

She took up her knitting and hurried home. There was the Straw Horse standing by the door with the Bear stuck to him.

'Old man, old man!' cried the old woman. 'Look, look! Our Straw Horse has brought us a Bear! Come and catch it!'

The old man sprang up, tore the Bear away from the Straw Horse, and put the Bear in the cellar.

Next morning the old woman again took her knitting and drove the Straw Horse out to graze. She sat herself down by a little hummock. She began to knit, and she sang:

> *'Graze, graze, little horse, in the sweet green grass,*
> *While I knit.*
> *Graze, graze, little horse, in the sweet green grass.'*

While she was knitting and singing she fell asleep.

Then out of the dark wood, out of the great forest, a grey Wolf came running and said to the Straw Horse, 'Who and what are you? Speak up now! Tell me!'

'I am a three-year-old horse, made of straw and smeared with tar,'

'If you are smeared with tar,' said the Wolf, 'then give me some tar too, so that I can smear my sides and the watch dogs will not bite me.'

'Take it,' said the Straw Horse.

The Wolf sprang at the side of the Straw Horse and tried to pull off the tar. He sank his teeth into the tar and pulled and pulled, but his jaws were stuck to the tar and he couldn't let go. He couldn't get away however much he fumed and struggled.

When the old woman woke up the Straw Horse was nowhere to be seen. 'Perhaps my Straw Horse has gone home,' she thought, and she went home too. There she saw the Straw Horse standing by the door with the Wolf stuck to him. She called her old man, and the old man put the Wolf in the cellar.

On the third day the old woman again drove the Straw Horse out to graze. She sat by a hillock and fell asleep. Then a Fox came running. 'Who and what are you?' he asked the Straw Horse.

'I am a three-year-old horse, made of straw and smeared with tar.'

'Give me some tar, my old dear,' said the Fox, 'and I will smear my sides lest those ugly greyhounds skin me.'

'Take it,' said the Straw Horse.

The Fox sprang and seized the tar with his jaws and couldn't let go.

The old woman woke up. She drove the Straw Horse home with the Fox still sticking to him. The old man put the Fox in the cellar with the Bear and the Wolf.

After that they caught a Hare too.

Now that they had all these creatures in the cellar, the old man sat down by the cellar door and began to sharpen his knife.

Then the Bear said, 'Old man, why are you sharpening your knife?'

'To skin you and make nice jackets from your fur, for me and my old woman.'

'Ah, don't skin me, old man! Let me go, and I will bring you honey.'

'All right then!'

The old man let the Bear go. Then he sat down again by the cellar door and began to sharpen his knife. '*Whim, whim, whim!*' went the knife.

Then the Wolf said, 'Old man, why are you sharpening that knife?'

'To skin you and make a warm jacket for the winter.'

'Ah, don't skin me, little grandfather! I will bring you a whole flock of sheep!'

'All right then.' And he let the Wolf go.

He sat down again and sharpened the knife. Then the Fox put out his little snout and said, 'Be so kind, grandfather, as to tell me, why you are sharpening that knife?'

'The Fox has a beautiful fur, just right for coat collars,' said the old man. 'So I am going to skin you.'

'Ah, don't take my skin off, grandfather dear! I will bring you geese and hens as well!'

'All right,' said the old man and he let the Fox go.

Only the Hare was left. The old man began to sharpen his knife again. The Hare asked him why and he said, 'The little Hare has a lovely soft warm fur, to make me warm gloves for the winter.'

'Ah, don't skin me, grandfather! I will bring you ribbons, earrings too, and lovely necklaces. Only let me go!'

The old man let the Hare go.

The old man and woman went to bed and slept through the night. Next morning just when the sun was rising, something scratched at the door, 'Durrr, durrr!'

The old woman woke up. 'Old man, old man! Someone's scratching at our door. Go and see who it is.'

The old man went out, and there was the Bear who had brought a hive full of honey. The old man thanked the Bear, put the honey in the larder and went back to bed. But no sooner had he lain down than again there was a scratching at the door, 'Durr-rr!' The old man looked out of the window and saw that the Wolf had driven a whole flock of sheep into the courtyard.

Soon after that came the Fox driving in flocks of geese, ducks and hens.

Last of all came the Hare bringing ribbons, earrings and lovely necklaces.

The old man was overjoyed and the old woman was overjoyed too. My word, they felt rich!

Then the Straw Horse said, 'You don't need me any more, so I'm going home.'

'Where is your home, my horse?' asked the old man.

'Ah ha! Wouldn't you like to know!' said the Straw Horse. And he kicked up his heels and galloped off. Nor did the old man or the old woman ever see him again.

7. *The Princess in the Iron Tower*

I How Baldwin found the Princess

Once upon a time a noble lady named Gertrude lived in a lonely old mansion-house under the mountains. Lady Gertrude had four sons. The two eldest, Otto and Adelbert, were away at the wars. The third son, Leopold, was a page at the court of the king of Bohemia; and only the youngest son, Baldwin, was still at home with his mother.

Lady Gertrude had a magic mirror. When she wanted to see how her sons were getting on, she only had to look in this mirror and say:

> *'Golden mirror, magic mirror,*
> *Without delaying, without staying,*
> *Show me what my sons are doing.'*

Then in the mirror she saw her two eldest sons, Otto and Adelbert, winning honours on the battlefield, and Leopold, her third son, in great favour at the court of the king of Bohemia.

Meanwhile her youngest son, Baldwin, who was still at home, had grown into a very handsome lad, and he longed to set out on knightly adventures. But Lady Gertrude was unwilling to let him go. 'Wait,' she said, 'Your time has not yet come.'

One day when Lady Gertrude looked in her magic mirror and asked to see her sons, she saw a huge dark forest where all kinds of wild animals were wandering sadly to and fro. What could this mean? Where were her sons? 'Show me my *sons*!' she said to the mirror. But all the mirror showed her was a beautiful white horse, and beside it a greyhound and a wolf. And as she watched, an elegant lady mounted the horse and rode away, chasing the wolf, and followed by the greyhound.

49

'But show me *Otto*, show me *Adelbert*, show me *Leopold*!' cried Lady Gertrude to the mirror. But the mirror only showed her the white horse, the greyhound, and the wolf.

Again and again Lady Gertrude asked the mirror to show her these three sons. And again and again the mirror showed her the forest, and the white horse, the greyhound, and the wolf; until at last Lady Gertrude realised that her three sons must have been changed into these three animals.

Then Lady Gertrude asked the mirror to show her where this forest was; and the mirror showed the eastern frontier of Bohemia, where a five-cornered iron tower stood by the roadside at the entrance to a great dark forest. And from a high window of the tower a most beautiful maiden was looking out.

Early next morning Lady Gertrude went to the sleeping Baldwin's bedside and shook him into wakefulness. 'My dear son,' she said, 'your ardent wish to set out on adventures has reached its fulfilment, and a high duty calls you away from your home.'

Then Baldwin sprang up joyfully from his bed, and his mother went on, 'Your brothers, oh my Baldwin, are in great trouble. Some evil power has turned one into a white horse, another into a greyhound, and the third into a wolf. And it is you who must deliver them. So show yourself worthy of such a valiant deed. Take the high road to the east, until you are on the other side of the frontier, where at the entrance of a wide and dark forest, you will find a high five-cornered iron tower. Wait there, and you will receive, from the hand of innocence, that which will protect you from all evil.'

Joyfully Baldwin began to dress, put on the shining armour that his careful mother had brought him, girded on the good sword which she had specially saved up for him, and after he had once more embraced his kind mother, and received her best blessing, he swung himself gaily upon the horse she had given him.

He rode, as his mother had instructed him, towards the east, and came at last to a great forest. At the entrance to the forest stood a high five-cornered tower of pure iron, which he recognised to be the very tower of which his mother had told him. Baldwin decided to stay here, and stepped into a tavern which stood by the roadside not far from the tower.

In the night he was lying awake in his bed in the tavern, wondering what he was to do next, when suddenly he heard a delightful sound of music, coming it seemed from not far off. So he got up, dressed and went out into the open air. There he heard quite distinctly, coming from the tower, the sweet voice of a girl singing to a lute. This is what she was singing:

> 'Now is the lovely month of May
> When the little flowers bloom in the vale;
> When the lark sweetly sings,
> And joyfully sings the nightingale.
>
> 'When the true lover once more
> Vows anew to the service of love.
> But I, unhappy, sit in captivity,
> Sit sadly and alone.
>
> 'If it were God's will,
> Then God's will be done;
> But chains of sorcery
> Are too heavy for me.
>
> 'And I see how outside comes the daylight,
> See how the night falls again.
> But for ever and for ever
> I am a prisoner here.
> No joy comes near me.'

Baldwin was greatly touched by this sorrowful song. He didn't doubt for a moment that it was his destiny to free this unhappy maiden and that he would receive from her hands the means to rescue his unfortunate brothers, too.

He listened for a long time after that, but the voice was silent. However often he called, with the kindest words, not another sound met his ears.

Baldwin watched and waited in vain the whole of the next day, the next night, and again the whole day - the lovely captive didn't appear. It

52

wasn't until the third night, when he was again roaming out in the open, that the maiden appeared on the battlement of the tower. Baldwin saw her white robe shimmering in the moonlight. He called to her, and besought her to tell him how he could set her free; because he would gladly venture his life to rescue her.

Greatly cheered by these kind words, the lovely maiden, whose name was Milada, bade him stand under the only window of the tower, and she would come down and talk to him from the window. Baldwin followed her bidding; and as he found an oak tree growing close to the tower beside the window, he climbed into the tree and swung himself lightly and nimbly from branch to branch, until he reached a branch close to the window itself. There he awaited the coming of the maiden, who was not a little astonished when she, by the light of the moon, saw the handsome youth so near her. He too was astonished at the beauty of Milada's face, which, though overlaid with the pallor of a deep sorrow, was yet wonderfully lovely.

Then cried Baldwin, 'Speak, lovely maiden! Tell me whether it is in my power to set you free, and what means I must use to this end?'

And Milada answered, 'I thank you, generous knight, but great as is my confidence in your valour, that valour alone will not suffice to free me, or to protect you, from the malignancy of a deceitful sorceress. Rather should you flee, oh handsome youth, before she lures you into her snare, and prepares for you a most cruel fate.'

But Baldwin answered, 'I am by no means so faint-hearted as to flee when danger threatens. I have made up my mind to free you; and if you will do me the honour to take me as your knight, I swear to you that I will not lay my head to rest until I have set you once more at liberty. Tell me, lovely maiden, who is the cruel one who has imprisoned you here?'

And Milada answered, 'As you insist on it, so I will tell you my sorrowful history. I am a princess of the royal family of Bohemia, and I was betrothed to my cousin, the son of the present king, when the wicked sorceress Ismainy, the owner of this enchanted forest, came from a distant land to the king's court, and fell in love with my betrothed. She declared to him her feelings, and left no means untried to win him away from me; but when she found that neither her beauty nor her skill were able to win him from me, her love turned to spite, which she vented on me. In the middle of the night the demons under her command seized me, and bore me through the air to this tower, where she, by her magic power, keeps me shut in. Here I have languished for many moons, and my betrothed has meanwhile died of grief at my loss.'

Then cried Baldwin, glowing with rage and indignation, 'Tell me, where is this heartless creature? Surely it is the very same who has turned my three brothers into animals, and so keeps them for herself.'

'Yes,' said Milada, 'it may well be so, because the forest is thronged with thousands of unhappy knights and prices whom the sorceress has turned into animals. But how will you alone vanquish her magic arts? Her beauty will ensnare you, like all the others – until you, too, will wander through the forest in the shape of a lion or a stag. But tell me, noble youth, who you are, and what has led you to this lamentable place?'

Baldwin told the princess what quest had brought him here. And when the princess saw that he was quite determined to go into the forest, and to compel the wicked sorceress to set her and his brothers free, she said, 'Since you will not be dissuaded from your intention, which is so noble and good that you surely have the protection of heaven, listen to me carefully. Go to the sorceress, Ismainy. Your handsome looks will win her heart – may God protect *your* heart! In two days the moon will be full, and at the full moon Ismainy must fall into a deep sleep that lasts for one hour – during that hour, nothing can wake her. Whilst Ismainy sleeps, all the animals in the enchanted forest take their human shapes once more, but without being able to leave the forest. When the sorceress wakes up, they turn back into animals. You will have just one hour to find your brothers. You might even have time to rob the sorceress of her power while she is asleep. Take this ring with the bright shining ruby. I was given it by my godmother, a powerful fairy, and if I hadn't forgotten to turn the stone inwards when Ismainy's demons seized me, the good fairy would have arrived to free me from their power. But she cannot enter this tower, and so this ring is no use to me here. Take it, it will protect you in danger, and may you return safely to the iron tower.'

At Baldwin's request, in taking leave, Milada reached him her tender hand through the iron grating, and he pressed a hearfelt kiss upon it, promising that he would soon return and would open the iron tower.

Then the princess drew back, and Baldwin climbed down from the tree and returned to the tavern, where he lay awake for the rest of the night, thinking of all he had to do.

II   Baldwin Meets Ismainy the Sorceress

At daybreak Baldwin left the tavern to seek out the sorceress Ismainy, and he hadn't walked very far into the forest when the sounds of a hunt fell on his ears; he heard the cheerful winding of the hunting horn, and the merry sound of the hunting-song ringing out of the thicket. Then he heard the dogs giving tongue, and the wild clamour of the hunt. From all sides pressed forward hunters and dogs, and girls in short skirts with the weapons of the hunt. A wolf bolted out of the thicket and stood quietly beside Baldwin almost as if it sought protection at his feet. Baldwin thought of the wolf that his mother had seen in her magic mirror, and he was looking compassionately down at the creature, when, following the fresh trail came a crowd of hunters and dogs, and at their head upon a snow-white thoroughbred, in an elegant hunting costume, was a beautiful woman whom Baldwin immediately guessed to be Ismainy, the sorceress, mistress of the forest.

Ismainy was as much astonished as overjoyed to find a young knight in her forest, the handsomest lad she had ever seen in her life. She received him in the kindest manner, and immediately invited him to accompany her to her palace. Baldwin was dazzled by her great beauty and he had to admit to himself that he had not expected so delightful an enemy. In fact, he might have fallen in love with her on the spot, if his heart had not been already full of love for the princess in the tower.

He accepted Ismainy's invitation, and, at his request, the wolf was permitted to run off unharmed into the bushes.

For two days Baldwin was entertained royally by the sorceress. When she asked him who he was and from whence he came, he told her that he was the son of a knight, that he had set out in search of adventure, and that he could never be sufficiently grateful for the chance that had led him to her forest.

Ismainy the sorceress was satisfied with this tale, and she made up her mind that she would keep this handsome youth with her for ever.

On the evening of the full moon, the sorceress, as the princess had told Baldwin, retired to her bedchamber to sleep for one hour. She asked Baldwin not to take it amiss that she must leave him for that hour; perhaps he would permit her maidens to try to shorten the time for him with songs and dances.

The maidens assembled in the great hall of the palace, and while some of them danced, others sang to the sound of the harp. But Baldwin was not cheered by their singing and dancing, and whilst they were all whirling round he left the hall, hurried into the dense forest, and ran up and down shouting out his eldest brother's name, 'Otto! Otto!' And at last Otto appeared, not as a white horse; because since the sorceress was asleep, Otto was now in his own handsome human form.

Otto told Baldwin how he and his two brothers, Adelbert and Leopold, had met the sorceress in three separate places. And how she had changed Adelbert into a greyhound, Leopold into a wolf, and he himself into the white horse which she usually rode.

'Alas!' cried Otto, 'how swiftly has the hour that Ismainy sleeps gone by! And I have so much more to tell you! But back to the palace, Baldwin! The sorceress must not miss you when she wakes, or you too will not escape her vengeance!'

Baldwin spoke a few words of comfort to the unhappy Otto, and then hurried back into the palace. He decided to stay here until the next full moon, when Ismainy would again sleep for one hour. And during that hour he hoped to find out from Otto what means he must use to overthrow Ismainy's power.

III   Baldwin Frees the Princess

The elegant sorceress, Ismainy, became day by day more delighted with her guest Baldwin. She felt that she could not live without him, and she offered him her hand in marriage, and a share of her power.

Baldwin pretended to consent to her wishes; but he insisted that they should put off their marriage for five weeks, because, he said, he had taken a vow that he would not marry until after his next birthday.

So came the time of the next full moon, and no sooner was Ismainy in her bedchamber than Baldwin plunged into the forest and sought out his brother Otto, who was astonished to hear that Baldwin was still free and that he had remained in his own shape after four weeks in the domain of the sorceress. Otto told Baldwin that all Ismainy's power lay in a golden key, and in a magic rose that never withered. 'This golden key,' Otto said, 'opens the door of the iron tower, and if the key is taken away from Ismainy, she will have no more power over the captives of the tower and the forest. Then all we, who are condemned to roam the forest in the shapes of animals, will regain our human forms.

'But while Ismainy has the rose a great deal of her power yet remains. With the rose she can change herself to any shape she pleases, and her demons still have to obey her.'

When Baldwin heard this he left his brother with the promise of a speedy deliverance, and hurried to Ismainy's bedchamber in order to rob her of her power. The sorceress lay asleep upon a magnificent couch, and beside her head, upon a richly embroidered cushion, lay the two talismans, the golden key and the magic rose.

Baldwin first snatched up the golden key so that he could free Milada, but then as he stretched his hand out to seize the magic rose, the hour ended. Ismainy awoke, snatched up the rose, leapt swiftly from her couch and waved the rose in the air.

At once the room was filled with flames. Ismainy's demons rushed upon Baldwin, who ran out of the room, and fled away through the halls of the palace, hotly pursued by Ismainy and her demons. Just in time, Baldwin remembered the magic ring that Milada had given him; he turned the ruby inwards and suddenly the good fairy appeared, bathed in a dazzling white light. Ismainy turned back appalled, and the demons sank powerless to the ground.

The good fairy congratulated Baldwin for ending the enchantment of the forest, and vanquishing the greater part of Ismainy's power. Ismainy had slipped away abashed. But, of course, she still had the magic rose.

Then the good fairy went with Baldwin to the iron tower. Baldwin unlocked the tower door with the golden key, Milada joyfully ran out, and with one word the good fairy turned the iron tower into a pile of dust. Then she handed Baldwin a pomegranate and said, 'Take this fruit which will never wither, and if at any time misfortune strikes you, then cut it open, that I may appear to comfort and help you.' And without waiting for Baldwin's thanks, the good fairy vanished.

Now shouting and cheering there came from the forest a great crowd of knights and princes, released from their animal shapes; and among them came Baldwin's three brothers, Otto, Adelbert, and Leopold. They were all riding their horses, which Ismainy the sorceress had turned into horseflies, but which now had regained their own shape.

Merrily turning their backs on the forest, they all set out for the court of the king of Bohemia. The king was overjoyed to see his lovely niece, Milada, again. And when he heard the whole story, the king made Baldwin an earl and honoured Baldwin's three brothers with positions at court.

IV Ismainy's Last Trick

Well now of course Baldwin married the lovely Milada and lived happily with her in the castle on his fine estate. By and by their joy was increased by the birth of their little son, whom they named Johann.

And looking every day into her magic mirror, Lady Gertrude saw with delight the happiness of all her sons.

But one day, when Lady Gertrude looked into her magic mirror and said:

> *'Golden mirror, magic mirror,*
> *Without delaying, without staying,*
> *Show me what my sons are doing.'*

the bright mirror showed her all her sons clearly in vivid colours. Only the images of Baldwin's wife and the baby Johann, she couldn't quite make out – they were faint and flickering, like wavering shadows on a windy day.

This troubled Lady Gertrude greatly, and at once she made up her mind to visit Baldwin, and see for herself if all was well with his wife and baby.

But when Lady Gertrude arrived at Baldwin's castle she felt a strange dislike both for Milada and the baby, a dislike she couldn't account for, and which in spite of all the pains she took she was quite unable to overcome.

Next day Lady Gertrude was sitting with Baldwin and Milada in a cosy little room in the castle. She had her grandson, baby Johann, on her lap. But the baby became restless and unruly. So Baldwin, to amuse the child, took up the pomegranate that the good fairy had given him, and began tossing it from one hand to the other. But Milada said she would like to taste the pomegranate. 'Then we will all share it,' said Baldwin. And he took a knife and cut the pomegranate.

But as Baldwin cut the pomegranate Milada vanished and Baldwin, to his horror, saw beside him Ismainy, the sorceress. And upon Lady Gertrude's lap, instead of a lovely baby boy, sat a hideous misshapen little demon with great horns and goat's feet, whom Lady Gertrude in terror shook off her lap.

The little demon fell sprawling on to the floor. Then the wall opened, the good fairy stepped out, and at her side came Milada with the real baby Johann in her arms.

'You see, Baldwin,' said the good fairy, 'I could not come until you summoned me by cutting the pomegranate. The wicked Ismainy's demons carried off Milada as she was walking with her baby in the garden. They dropped her in the wilderness, but I took her into my palace. Meanwhile Ismainy had taken on the shape of Milada, and had changed one of her demons into the shape of your little son Johann. But now I promise you that she shall trouble you no more. I will banish her to an underground cavern, where, rage as she will, she can do no further harm.'

After that all went well. Lady Gertrude left her lonely mansion house under the mountains, and came to live with Baldwin. And in Baldwin's castle, he, his mother, his wife, and his little son Johann, lived happily ever after.

8. *Malegy's Palfrey*

One summer evening three pretty girls, Magdalen and Lucia and Mixima, were taking a walk along a country lane near the town of Ypres. The girls were not sisters, but they all lived near each other, and they were great friends.

Well, there they were, rambling along and chatting of this and that, when, rounding a corner of the lane, they saw standing before them, right in the middle of the lane, a chestnut horse. The horse was saddled and bridled; and – my word – he was a beauty! His body so shapely, his coat so smooth and sleek, his mane and tail shining in the sunset light like pure gold.

'Oh you lovely, lovely creature!' cried Magdalen. 'How I would love to be up on your back!'

'And so would I!' cried Lucia.

'And so would I!' cried Maxima.

'Well then, why not?' the horse seemed to be saying. For he moved over against the hedge, where some small flowering bushes and a few boulders made climbing easy.

Then Magdalen scrambled up into the saddle. Lucia scrambled up behind Magdalen. Maxima scrambled up behind Lucia. And 'Off we go, my beauty!' cried Magdalen, giving a slap to the reins.

And off trotted the chestnut horse.

At first he was going at a slow trot; then he was going at a canter, then he was going at a gallop. The girls were laughing, the girls were singing, the girls were calling out, 'Gee up! Gee up!' They weren't heeding a bit where the horse was taking them; nor were they heeding that the sun had gone down behind the hills, and that twilight was coming on, and that dark clouds were gathering in the sky.

And then Lucia looked up at the sky and said, 'Don't you think we'd better turn back?'

'Yes, perhaps we'd better,' said Magdalen. And she gave a pull at the left-hand rein.

Oh ho! The chestnut horse wasn't taking any notice of *that*! The horse knew where he was going: and that was straight on.

And on he went and on, galloping now so fast that the world seemed to be flying back behind him; when, suddenly turning a corner, he came to a place where light streamed out across the road from innumerable windows. And there he stopped with a jerk before the gates of a magnificent palace.

The palace windows were wide open, and through them came the sound of music and the *trip, trip, trip* of hundreds of dancing feet. With a toss of his nose the horse pushed open the gates, trotted sedately across the courtyard, and came to a stand before a great golden door.

Immediately the door was flung wide, and out came a little crowd of elegantly-dressed ladies.

'Welcome Magdalen, welcome Lucia, welcome Maxima!' cried the elegantly-dressed ladies. 'We are having such a merry time, and we are delighted to see you! Come and join in the fun!'

Now the elegantly-dressed ladies were helping the girls to scramble off the horse's back: now, one on either side of each girl, they were holding the girls' hands, and leading them through the great golden door. Now they were bringing them into a dance hall, where the musicians had ceased to play, and the dancers had ceased to dance, and were standing back against the walls. For a moment there was not a sound to be heard. And then two big doors at the farther end of the dance hall were flung open, and in came the lord of the palace. He was dressed in a ruby red damask robe, and on his head he wore a turban that glittered with diamonds.

'Welcome Magdalen, welcome Lucia, welcome Maxima,' said the lord of the palace, stepping up to the three girls. 'We are about to sit down to supper, and we have three places reserved for you. Come, follow me.'

And he led them into another room, where a long table was spread with all sorts of delicious things to eat and drink. The crowd of dancers followed after them: and the whole company sat down to supper.

Well, well, by this time the girls were so astonished that it seemed they must be dreaming. But certainly the food and the wine were real enough. The girls were hungry after their long ride, and they ate and drank heartily. And when the supper came to an end, the lord of the palace, who sat at the head of the table, stood up and spoke in a loud, clear voice. This is what he said:

'Ladies and gentlemen, now that Malegy's palfrey has procured for us the very great pleasure of receiving into our house these three young ladies from Ypres, we must see to it that they pass the evening pleasantly. I propose that we play a game of forfeits.'

Lucia looked doubtfully at Maxima; Maxima looked doubtfully at Magdalen. Magdalen pushed back her chair, got to her feet, and said shyly:

'My lord, it is very, very kind of you, and we have enjoyed ourselves very much; but I fear that our parents will be getting anxious, and I think it is time we went home.'

'Yes, yes, it is really time we went home!' echoed Lucia and Maxima.

Oh dear me, hardly had they spoken those words when the smile on the face of the lord of the palace vanished. Now he was scowling, and his eyes flashed so angrily that he looked like the very devil himself. The three girls were too frightened to say anything more, and without another word, they went with the rest of the company into a room where small tables were laid out with packs of cards. The girls sat down at one of these tables with the lord of the palace, who, rapidly explaining the rules of the game, dealt out the cards with lightning speed, and with lightning speed began to play. But the girls, utterly confused by the rapidity of the game, lost time after time. And every time they lost they must pay a forfeit.

First they paid with their rings, then they paid with their bracelets, then they paid with their ear-rings, then they paid with their pretty shoes, and then they paid with their stockings. And still it seemed that they must go on playing, and still they must go on losing: until they had nothing left to pay with, except their clothes. So, by and by, there they were utterly ashamed, each one sitting with nothing on but her chemise.

Then the lord of the palace laughed, rose to his feet, and said, 'Ladies and gentlemen, our games for the night are now ended. But before we part, let us drink to the health of Malegy's Palfrey, who has so graciously brought these three young ladies to our palace.'

'Malegy's Palfrey! Malegy's Palfrey!' The cry re-echoed through the room. And as the lord of the palace raised his glass his appearance began to change: his eyes flashed fire, his lips snarled, and out of his head sprouted four great horns. And the terrified girls were lifted up by a great wind, and whirled out of the palace and round and round, and dumped down at last on the dewy grass of a green valley among high surrounding hills.

Oh what unfortunate girls! Now they were shedding tears. It was Magdalen who first dried her eyes. 'What has happened, has happened, and can't be helped,' she said. 'Come, we musn't sit here blubbering like babies. It is our business to find our way home.'

So they all got up and walked on. It was night, and the stars were glittering in a cloudless sky. And by and by they came to a cottage and knocked at the door.

A man opened the door and stared at them in astonishment. And well he might be astonished. For it is not often that you see by lantern light three girls standing at your door, each with nothing on but a chemise.

'Wh-what do you want, and wh-where have you come from?' he stammered.

Then they told him of their strange adventure, and he said, 'Ah, seems as if you'd been in the clutches of them blanketty, blanketty sorcerers, and indeed of Old Nick himself. We hear their goings-on every night. Only an hour agone the racket they were making roused me from my bed. I got up and put my head out of the window. But I could see nought save a great light. Yet I heard music and singing and the *trip-a-trip* of dancing feet . . . But I don't know as I can help you,' he said, looking at the girls in a scared kind of way. 'How do I know,' he was thinking, 'whether these three raggety-looking females may not be members of the devilish gang, come here to do a mischief to my good wife and me?'

And as he was so thinking, his wife's voice cried out from an upstairs room: 'No, no, Klaes, don't you give them anything! Our baby's screaming murder, and that's a sure sign as this is devil's work! Quick, quick, shut and bolt the door, before them three witches snatch our baby from us!'

The man, now thoroughly scared, slammed the door. And the three disconsolate girls wandered on under the stars, footsore, weary, and not knowing in the least which way to take to find the road that should bring them home.

'Oh *why* did we ever get up on that horse's back?' wailed Lucia.

'And why, *why*, did we ever go into that accursed palace?' sobbed Maxima.

'And why, why, *why* did we ever sit down to play cards with the devil?' cried Magdalen. 'But look, here we are now at the bottom of the valley, and here is a broad road, and here is an inn. Perhaps the innkeeper can direct us which way we should go. But we won't tell him about Malegy's Palfrey — he'd never believe us. We must make up some more real-sounding tale.'

So she knocked at the door of the inn. And when the innkeeper opened the door, Magdalen told him that they had been set upon by thieves, and had been robbed of all their trinkets, and also of their clothes.

'I know it was very naughty of us to go wandering out into the country at night by ourselves,' she said. 'But I assure you we've learned our lesson, and we shan't do it again.' Then she told him that they lived in the town of Ypres, and she told him the names of their parents.

'Why, bless my soul!' said the innkeeper. 'I know your fathers well! Many a time they have dropped in here to refresh themselves. If that's how it is, I best get out my wagon, harness in my horses, and drive you home, for your people will be in a rare taking! And, my days, I best loan you some blankets to wrap yourselves up in, for upon my word — well —'

'Oh I know, I know,' sobbed Magdalen, 'you needn't tell me we're not fit to be seen!'

'It's certainly not the way young ladies usually go about,' said the inn-keeper. And then he burst out laughing. And that made the girls see that their adventure had a funny side to it, and they cheered up.

So, whilst the innkeeper went to get out his wagon and harness in his two horses, the girls went into the inn and sat by the fire. The innkeeper's wife brought them each a blanket and a cup of hot coffee, for both of which they were very grateful, for they were shivering with cold. And in less than half an hour the wagon, with its two big horses, stood ready at the inn door. The girls scrambled up into the wagon, the innkeeper took his seat in front of them, and with a jerk of the reins and a '*Yip, yip, yip, my hearties!*' off they went.

The innkeeper knew the road that led to the town of Ypres, as well as he knew the back of his own hand; but somehow on that very early morning he lost his way. And to his utter astonishment, he suddenly found himself, wagon and all, going along through the middle of a field.

'This is most peculiar!' he said. And he tried to turn round to get back to the high road. But the horses refused to turn round; they were galloping now over hedge and ditch, across dykes, through thickets, and over ploughed land, with the wagon bumping and jolting and all but upsetting, the innkeeper shouting and tugging at the reins, and the terrified girls clutching at the sides of the wagon to prevent themselves from being flung out.

'Oh look, look!' cried Magdalen. 'Look at that shadowy horse gliding along before us! I know what that is — it's Malegy's Palfrey! It's that horse that's leading us astray again! Oh what can we do? What *can* we do?'

'We can do nothing,' panted the innkeeper. 'We must let the horses have their heads and wait for dawn. See, even now the east is reddening.'

So on they went at that mad gallop, bump, bump, *bump*! But when the sun rose, the shadowy shape of Malegy's Palfrey vanished, and the innkeeper's horses quietened down. Now they were trotting sedately along a broad high road.

'But I'm blessed if I know where we are!' said the innkeeper. Then he saw a lad with a flock of sheep coming towards them, and he pulled up.

'Hey, boy, can you tell me the road to Ypres?'

The lad stared. '*Ypres*!' he said. 'You're more than two hours' distance from it, not to mention that you're on the wrong road. You must go back and turn to the right at the cross-roads.'

'Oh heavens!' cried Magdalen. 'Why did we ever get on to the back of that wretched horse?'

'Well there, don't take on, young lady,' said the innkeeper kindly. 'I doubt you couldn't help yourselves. And after all,' he chuckled, 'it'll give you something to talk about for the rest of your lives.'

Then he drove back to the cross-roads, and there turned right as the shepherd lad had directed, and came, some two hours later, safely to Ypres, where the girls found their parents quite distracted, and all the neighbours out searching for them.

Of course the girls got a good scolding. Of course they shed tears, and promised never to do such a foolish thing again. And of course the innkeeper was thanked and rewarded, and drove home smiling to himself, with a nice sum of money in his pocket, and an interesting tale to tell his wife.

9. What Came of Quarrelling

Once upon a time there was a poor peasant who saved up a little money and bought a small field. He sowed the field with seeds of pumpkins, beans and spinach. All the seeds came up and the plants grew green and strong.

One day the peasant went out to look at his field. As he went into the field he heard a pumpkin say: 'Here comes the master of the field, ho, ho!'

And a bean said, 'Why don't you try to better yourself, you poor devil of a peasant?'

And the spinach said, 'Strike your stick upon the ground, peasant!'

But the peasant was frightened. He ran out of the field. He met a neighbour and said, 'Come quickly into my field, there is something very odd going on there!'

So the neighbour went with the peasant into the field. And the plants began to speak again.

'Here comes the master of the field, ho, ho!' said the pumpkin.

'Why don't you try to better yourself, you poor devil of a peasant?' said the bean.

'Strike your stick upon the ground, peasant!' cried the spinach.

So then the neighbour struck his stick upon the ground.

What happened? The ground opened, and out trotted a throng of glossy, golden arab mares with their foals running at their heels.

'Oh!' cried the peasant overjoyed. 'Just think — all these horses are mine! Now I am a rich man!'

'What are you talking about?' said the neighbour. 'They are not your horses, they are mine! It was I who called them up.'

'But it's my field,' said the peasant, 'and everything that comes out of my ground of course belongs to me.'

So they argued, and began quarrelling, and almost came to fisticuffs. Until at last the peasant said, 'Well this won't do. We must go and put our case before the king.'

So that's what they did. The king listened with astonishment, and then he said, 'This is a most extraordinary tale. I must come and see these animals for myself.'

So the king went with the peasant and the neighbour to the field. And there were the mares and the foals all standing quietly.

The king and the two men went into the field and the king said, 'Are you telling me that these beautiful animals really came up out of this ground? I can't believe it!'

Then the pumpkin said, 'You see, the king doesn't believe it. Ho, ho!'

The bean said, 'I told the master to better himself, but the neighbour came poking his nose in!'

And the spinach said, 'So you see it was the neighbour who struck the ground and not the master.'

'That's right,' said the neighbour. 'It was *I* who struck the ground – just like this.' And he struck the ground with his stick.

And then what happened? The ground opened again, and all the mares and all the foals trotted down into the ground and vanished.

The ground closed once more.

The neighbour struck the ground with his stick again and again. But would the ground open? No, it wouldn't, not it!

And the king said, 'Now, you silly fellows, you see what comes of quarrelling!'

10. Franz the Garden Boy

I The White Mare

Once upon a time there was a lad, called Franz, who went tramping through the world, looking for work. And on the top of a high hill he came to a castle. He knocked at the castle door, the door opened, and out hopped a little old man.

'What do you want?' said the little old man.

'A job of work,' said Franz.

'Well, if you'll work for me,' said the little old man, 'you'll get good wages: twenty pounds a week for the first year, fifty pounds a week for the second year, a hundred pounds a week for the third year, beside bed and board. What do you say?'

'I say yes, yes, and yes again!' said Franz.

So Franz took service with the little old man, whose name was Hermanni.

Franz worked hard and he worked well. He scrubbed and he polished, he had everything shining; he fetched in wood for the kitchen fire, he cooked the meals. There was food in plenty in the castle, though Franz could never make out where it came from. But what he liked best was to groom and tend a beautiful white mare, who lived in a stable at the back of the castle. This mare was magic. She could speak like a human being, and she and Franz had many happy conversations together.

Well, at the end of the first year, Franz asked for his wages. But the little old man, Hermanni, said, 'No hurry about *them*. You'll get them next year.'

So, having worked for a second year, Franz again asked for his wages. And Hermanni said, 'Oh bother the wages! You'll get them all at the end of the third year.'

71

So Franz worked for yet a third year, and then again he asked for his wages.

Well, he didn't get them, and you can be sure that vexed him. He couldn't make up his mind whether to go or stay, but he thought perhaps he'd better stay, at any rate until he got his wages. Every evening he was asking for those wages, and every evening Hermanni said, 'What a plague you are, you and your wages! Don't you get bed and board, don't you get food in plenty, haven't I given you a soft bed and a new suit of clothes? Why, a prince might envy the life you live with me!'

'But if I were to leave you, I shouldn't have anything,' said Franz.

'Then you better not leave me,' said Hermanni.

And he got very angry, and danced about, shaking his little fists. Soon after that, Hermanni told Franz that he was going away for a day or two, and that whilst he was away Franz must clean out all the rooms in the castle, except one room that was always kept locked.

'I'd like to know what's in that room,' said Franz.

'Well you can't,' said Hermanni.

'But why not?' said Franz.

'Because curiosity killed the cat,' said Hermanni, 'and maybe other things, besides cats.'

Next morning Hermanni went away. He was away a long time, and in that long time Franz set about cleaning out all the rooms from attic to cellar; except, of course, the locked room. He was getting more and more curious about that locked room, and one day he asked the white mare what was in it. And she said, 'Nothing at all – it's empty.' So then Franz said, 'Then why is it kept locked?' and the mare said, 'A man has a right to lock up his rooms if he wants to. And I'd advise you to think no more about it.'

But Franz did think more about it, and when he had cleaned all the other rooms in the castle, and still Hermanni didn't come back, he said to himself, 'If I could find the key of that room, I'd just take one little peep – there couldn't be any harm in just taking one little peep!' And he began searching for the key.

Well, he found the key: he found it in an unlikely place – inside the toe of one of Hermanni's cast-off shoes – and all excited he unlocked the door of that room to take his 'little peep'. But, would you believe it, the room was completely empty!

What a sell! Franz was laughing at himself now. He thought it must be just a silly joke on Hermanni's part . . . But what was this? The room was filled with a very sweet smell, as if all the most fragrant roses in the world were heaped up there. And yet there was nothing in it – nothing!

Franz sniffed and stared, sniffed and stared. Then a little breeze blew through the room. It was this little breeze that was filling the room with scent; and the breeze was coming from under another door at the end of the room. Franz went over to this other door: no, it wasn't locked. He turned the handle, opened the door, and stepped through into a garden.

And what a garden! Such a garden as surely was never seen on earth before. It was planted with glittering bushes; and well might those bushes glitter, for every twig and every leaf was diamond or gold or silver.

Oh, oh! Franz was running from one bush to another. He picked a little sprig from a diamond bush, he picked a little sprig from a golden bush, he picked a little sprig from a silver bush. He wrapped the little sprigs up in his handkerchief, and put the handkerchief in his pocket. Then he hurried from the garden, back into the empty room, and out of the empty room. He locked the door of the empty room behind him, and put the key again where he had found it – in the toe of one of Hermanni's cast-off shoes. Then he went to the stable to groom and feed the white mare.

Sniff, sniff, sniff, went the white mare's nostrils. 'Franz, where have you been, and what have you got in your pocket?'

'You'd never guess,' said Franz.

And he took his handkerchief out of his pocket, and showed her the three little glittering sprigs.

'Franz, Franz,' cried the mare, 'oh Franz, what have you done? Hermanni will be furious! And don't you comfort yourself with the belief that because he's so small you can hold your own against him. You can't. He has magic powers. He'll put a spell upon you! Heaven only knows what evil shape he'll turn you into! Run, fetch some food for yourself and come back to me. We must get away from here before Hermanni comes home!'

So Franz hurried into the castle, snatched up some bread and cheese and a bottle of wine, and came running out into the stable again, unloosed the mare, scrambled on to her back, and off she went, galloping, galloping.

Well, they hadn't gone far when they saw Hermanni on his way home,

coming along the road towards them. As soon as he saw them, he let out a hideous screech and began to run. The mare leaped over a gate into a field and galloped on. Hermanni scrambled over the gate and gave chase. He was fairly whizzing along on his little bandy legs. The mare jumped over another gate into another field. Hermanni scrambled over that gate. You'd think he had wings, the rate he was going.

'Don't look round, Franz,' panted the mare, 'but throw the whip behind you.'

So Franz threw the whip behind him. The whip turned into a high hedge, bristling with thorns. It took Hermanni a long time to get through that hedge. But get through it he did, and now he was coming on again, whizzing over the ground on his little bandy legs, and screaming and cursing.

'Quick, quick, Franz,' panted the mare; 'loosen the saddle strap and throw the saddle behind you!'

So Franz threw the saddle behind him, and the saddle turned into a great range of mountains, so high that their heads were lost in the clouds.

But in a long time, or a short time, and in a shorter time than you'd ever believe, Hermanni was up those mountains and down the other side of them, and here he was, whizzing along on his little bandy legs faster than fast, and gaining on the mare.

The mare was gasping and sweating, and covered with foam.

'Gather up the foam from my neck in your two hands and throw it behind you, Franz,' she panted.

So Franz did that, and the foam turned into a great sea. The billows of the sea rose high and white; their roaring and pounding filled the air. No, Hermanni couldn't cross that sea. He turned and went home, and his angry screams were drowned in the uproar of the waves.

'That was a narrow escape, Franz,' said the mare. 'But now we are safe. We will go on leisurely until we find some pleasant place where we can rest.'

So they travelled on leisurely, and by and by came to a charming green grove surrounded by huge old oak trees.

There they stopped. Franz slid from the mare's back, took off her bridle to give her more ease, and then sat down under an oak to eat his bread and cheese and drink his wine. It was very quiet there in that green grove. The only sounds were the light movements of the mare's hoofs and the little champing of her teeth as she pulled up and ate the grass . . .

And by and by Franz fell asleep.

When he woke, what was his surprise to find a table at his side; and on the table a bright-gleaming, naked sword.

'Franz,' said the mare, coming up close to him, 'I think I have saved your life?'

'I think so too, my mare.'

'And are you grateful, Franz?'

'I am more than grateful, my mare.'

'Then, Franz, will you do something for me?'

'Anything I can do, my mare.'

'Then, Franz, take that sword and cut off my head.'

'Oh no, no, *no*, my mare!'

'Franz, you have promised.'

'Oh I know, but anything else, my mare, anything but that!'

'Franz, that is the first and last thing I ask of you. And if you will not do it, I must go back to Hermanni; and if he does not kill me, he will surely beat me till I drop.'

'Oh my mare, my mare!'

Well, that's the way they were going on for a long time: Franz saying no he couldn't, and no he wouldn't cut off the mare's head, and she begging and praying him to do so, and then getting angry and stamping her feet, because he wouldn't, and then begging him and praying him again — yes, and actually sobbing — until he felt half-mad, and in desperation snatched up the sword.

One swing of the sword — the head was off; and Franz flung himself on the ground and covered his face with his hands. It was he who was sobbing now.

'Franz, Franz, Franz,' said a laughing voice. 'Look up, my dear, look up!'

Franz looked up — what did he see? A lovely lady dressed in white flowing robes, standing beside him.

'Franz,' said the lovely lady, 'I am a fairy princess, and I possess some magic. But my magic is not as powerful as Hermanni's. And because I would often try to thwart him in his evil doings, he turned me into the white mare. But now you have freed me, and now I must leave you. But first I will reward you.' And she broke off a little stick from an old hollow oak tree. 'Whenever you need my help, come to this hollow oak and strike on it with the little stick . . . . And now goodbye.'

Then the hollow oak opened. The fairy gathered up her white flowing robes and stepped inside the oak. The oak closed again. And Franz stood alone in the green glade.

II   The Princess

So Franz put the little stick in his pocket; and walking on, very soon came to a city. In the city there was a palace, in the palace lived a king, and behind the palace was a market garden. Franz went to the garden and asked if there was work there for an honest lad.

Yes, the gardener wanted such a lad. So Franz took service with him.

Well, one day the gardener was laid up with rheumatics, and Franz was working alone in the vegetable garden, hoeing among the cabbages. 'Poor things,' said he to the cabbages, 'how dull you look! Every leaf the same green, with no brightness or sparkle on you. How different from the plants in Hermanni's garden! Now they were really worth looking at! I'll show you!'

He took his handkerchief from his pocket, and unwrapped the three sprigs: the diamond sprig, the gold sprig, and the silver sprig that he had picked in Hermanni's garden.

'Wouldn't you like to look as pretty as that, and wouldn't you like to smell as sweetly?' said he. And he began drawing the sprigs to and fro over the heads of the cabbages.

Immediately there were the cabbages, one silver, one gold, one sparkling like a diamond, and scenting all the air with their sweet perfume.

Now it so happened that the princess, the king's young daughter, was looking out of a window in the palace; and from the window she could see the vegetable garden. She saw the rows of cabbages, and she saw Franz stooping among them, and all at once she saw those rows of cabbages lit up and sparkling like jewels. So she summoned a page and said, 'Go into the garden and tell the lad who is working there to bring me a basketful of young peas.'

The page went; and Franz picked the peas and carried them to the princess. And on his way he picked a daisy and stroked it with the silver sprig.

'Good day, princess.'

'Good day, garden boy.'

'Here I bring you a basketful of young peas.'

'Thank you, garden boy. That's a very lovely flower you have in your buttonhole, garden boy.'

'Oh that! That's only a daisy. You can have it.'

'Thank you, garden boy. And what do I owe you for the peas?'

'A hundred shillings.'

'Here you are, garden boy.'

'Thank you, princess. Goodbye for now, princess.'

'Goodbye, garden boy. I shall treasure this silver daisy.'

Franz went away then. He went to the gardener and gave him the hundred shillings.

'But, my dear lad,' said the gardener, 'a hundred shillings for a basket of peas! That's *much* too much!'

'Well, that's what she gave me,' said Franz.

So the gardener gave Franz fifty shillings for himself; and Franz bought himself a new cap with a feather in it.

The princess put the silver daisy in a vase. She kept looking at it and wondering. 'There's some mystery here!' she said to herself. And after she had puzzled her head about that mystery for a day or two, she again summoned the page.

'Go into the garden and tell the lad who is working there to bring me a basketful of roses,' she said.

So the page went, and Franz picked the roses and carried them to the princess. And on the way he stroked one rose with the silver sprig, and another rose with the gold sprig, and another with the diamond sprig. So there they were now: a silver rose, and a golden rose, and a diamond rose. And though those three roses had smelled sweet enough before, the scent of them now was ravishing.

'Good day, princess.'

'Good day, garden boy.'

'Here I bring you roses, princess.'

'Thank you, garden boy — oh how they glitter, these three roses, and how sweetly they smell! But are you hungry, garden boy?'

'Well, I could do with a snack.'

So the princess rang her bell and ordered cake and wine to be brought. Franz ate and drank heartily, and grew merry. And when the princess asked him as a great favour to tell her how he had magicked the three roses, he laughed, took the three sprigs from his pocket, and told her all about them. And then he ate some more, and drank some more, and his eyes kept closing, and his head kept nodding. And after a bit, there he was with his head on the table, sound asleep . . .

And the princess took the three sprigs out of his pocket, and locked them up in a drawer.

By and by, she was shaking him to wake him up.

'Time to go home, garden boy.'

'Yes, princess.'

'And how much do I owe you for the roses, garden boy?'

'Two hundred shillings, princess.'

'Here you are, garden boy.'

'Thank you, princess. Goodbye for now, princess.'

'Goodbye, garden boy. I shall treasure my roses!'

Franz went away then, and took the two hundred shillings to the gardener, who was feeling better, and sitting up in a chair.

'But, my lad,' said he, 'two hundred shillings for a basket of roses! I never heard of such a thing!'

'Well, that's what she gave me.'

So the gardener gave Franz a hundred shillings for himself.

Franz was pleased. He thought he would buy himself a silk shirt for Sundays. He went into the garden again. He was planning to amuse himself with the three sprigs: he'd brighten up a few more vegetables, and perhaps a bush or two. He put his hand in his pocket to take out the sprigs . . . But the sprigs were gone! Oh, the sprigs were gone! Perhaps he had dropped them? He ran about looking. He couldn't find them anywhere! He stamped and raved! He went to bed in a rage, he got up next morning in a rage. And when he heard that the princess had again sent for him, to bring her some vegetables, he bundled a few peas and cabbages into a basket, and went to her scowling.

'Here are your vegetables,' said he, with no manners at all.

'Thank you, garden boy. Sit down and eat, garden boy.'

'*No!*'

'Well, well, why so surly this morning?' says she.

'My sprigs have gone,' says he.

'You don't say so!' says she laughing.

'And if it's you that's taken them,' says he, 'I'll – I'll – '

'Well, what will you do?'

'Wring your neck,' he mutters. But not very loud.

'Come on then, wring it, wring it!' says she. 'Because I did take them. And you shall have them back for just one kiss.'

No, he wouldn't kiss her. But she gave him back his sprigs, all the same.

'And now you shall come to the king, my father,' says she.

And she took him by the hand and led him to the king.

'Daddy,' says she, 'I'm bringing you the greatest artist in all the world!'

'Is that so?' says the king. 'Well, let him show his skill.'

So then the princess cleared a big table, and Franz took his sprigs and painted the table all over with patterns of gold and silver and diamonds. The king was astonished. He gave Franz a bag of money and sent him away.

And when Franz had gone, the princess said, 'Daddy, I want to marry that lad.'

The king said, 'Rubbish!'

'No, it isn't rubbish,' said the princess. 'I love him, and if I can't have him, I won't have anybody. I'll live and die an old maid.'

Well, the king saw she meant it, and he wasn't going to have his dear daughter living and dying an old maid. So after a day or two he sent for Franz and said, 'Will you marry the princess?'

And Franz said, 'That I will!'

'But, my son,' says the king, 'you must have a palace. You can't marry without one.' (He was being cunning. He thought Franz not having a palace would put an end to the matter.)

80

But Franz said, 'If I haven't a palace today, I'll have one tomorrow.' And he bowed to the king very stiffly, and went away.

Where did he go? He went to the hollow oak in the green grove. He took the little stick that the fairy had given him, and struck with it on the hollow tree.

Out comes the fairy.

'God's blessing on you, Franz! What are you wishing?'

'I am wishing to marry the king's daughter. But the king says I must first have a palace. Please, how can I get a palace? I have no money to build one.'

So then the fairy gave Franz a little purse with a few gold coins in it. 'It looks small,' said she 'but it holds much. You can take as many gold pieces as you like out of it. It will never be empty.'

'Oh thank you, dear fairy!'

And there was Franz running back to the king again.

'Now I have money,' says he. 'Now I can begin to build.'

And he shows the king the little purse.

'But, my son, the money in that little purse won't build a palace!'

'I think there's more gold in this purse than in all your treasury,' says Franz. And he opens the purse, holds it upside down over the table, and gives it a shake.

Out come the gold coins chinking and tinkling; and out they come and out they come, till the table's piled high with them – and then Franz shouts with laughter, and shakes out more gold coins all over the floor. Now he's ankle-deep in gold, and the king is gasping and staring.

'That's enough, that's enough!' cries the king. 'I never met with such a fellow in all my life!'

Now the king's laughing as well as Franz. And he gave Franz a piece of land, and told him to go ahead and build his palace.

So Franz hired workmen and set about building. He was shaking out gold from the purse every day, buying this and that. And when the palace was built and furnished, it was even finer that the king's own palace.

'So now we can hold the wedding,' said Franz.

'Oh no, we can't!' cried the king. 'I'm up to the neck in trouble – and it's all your fault! You see, I'd as good as promised the princess in marriage to King Moydor, my neighbour, and now she says she won't marry him because of you. So he's raising an army to come and fetch her, and he has twice as many fighting men as I have, and oh dear, dear, I don't know what to do!'

'No need to worry,' says Franz. 'I'll take care of that.'

And off he goes to the green grove and strikes the hollow oak with his little stick.

Out comes the fairy. 'God's blessing on you, Franz! What is it this time?'

'Oh dear fairy, King Moydor is coming to do battle with our king, and King Moydor's army is twice the size of ours. Help me please!'

So then the fairy gives Franz a sword. 'When you come near the battlefield,' says she, 'you'll see an oak tree growing by the way – a mighty oak tree, much like this one. Strike the oak with your sword and soldiers will march out of it – horse-soldiers and foot-soldiers, just as many as you need.'

'Thank you, dear fairy! Goodbye, dear fairy!'

Franz went back to the king and found him reviewing his troops. He had called up every man in the kingdom, rich and poor, sick and well.

'What are all these people doing?' says Franz. 'Why are they gathered together?'

'To fight, my boy, to fight,' says the king. 'And there aren't nearly enough of them. But we can only fight and die.'

'There are far too many of them!' says Franz. 'Let all the married men go home, for I think their wives are weeping, and their children crying. Send home all the old men too. Leave this war to me. I know how to manage it.'

'Well, if you say so, my boy,' answered the king. And he was thinking, 'If we're beaten, this tiresome Franz will be taken prisoner, or may be even killed. And then my daughter will marry King Moydor, and everything will be happily settled.'

So he sent home all the volunteers, and kept only his small regular army, which immediately set out against the enemy, with the king and Franz riding at their head.

When they came near the battlefield – my goodness, there was King Moydor's army, soldiers upon soldiers, as far as the eye could reach, nothing but soldiers, horse and foot, with their weapons flashing, and their drums beating, and all the air ringing with the clamour of fifes and drums and trumpets.

'It's high time we ourselves got more soldiers,' says Franz to the king.

'But from where, from where?' cried the king.

'Now, now, dear father, don't excite yourself,' says Franz. 'Just you draw aside, and keep clear of that oak tree you see growing over there, so that my soldiers won't tumble over you.'

And he went to the oak tree and struck it with his sword.

What happened? The oak tree opened, and out from it soldiers came pouring, regiment upon regiment of horse-soldiers, and regiment upon regiment of foot-soldiers, and regiment upon regiment of artillery with cannon. In no time at all, they had set upon King Moydor's troops and driven them back and back, until only a few scattered soldiers of the enemy were left on the battlefield, and those few were fleeing in all directions.

And see! The victorious regiments that Franz had summoned out of the oak are all trooping back into the oak again. The oak tree closes behind them, and the king, the princess's father, is shouting 'Victory! Victory!' He is half-crazy with joy; he is jumping off his horse to embrace Franz as his 'dear, dear son and heir . . .!'

And so, of course, Franz married the princess, and with her lived happily ever after.

11. Master Billy

Once upon a time there was a poor man who lived in a cottage all by himself, and his name was Zach Penbeagle.

Well, one cold night, as Zach was sitting over the fire, there came a knock at the door.

Zach went to open it, and there stood a little, small dwarfie of a boy, wearing a red cap.

'Shall I come my ways in?' said the little, small dwarfie.

'Why yes, if you've a mind to,' said Zach. 'But we'll shut fast the door, for 'tis a draughty old night, to be sure.'

So the little, small dwarfie stepped in, and Zach shut the door fast, and the dwarfie sat down by the fire.

'I don't know as I've the pleasure of your acquaintance?' said Zach.

'No,' said the dwarfie, 'you don't know me, but I know you, and I'm thinking you're not so well off as some folks?'

'I don't complain,' said Zach. 'But I'll own I could do with a bit more.'

'Well now, you listen close to what I'm going to tell you,' said the dwarfie. 'And if I don't put you in the way of getting a big bag of gold, my name's not Master Billy.'

'Might that be your name then?' said Zach.

'I wouldn't say it wasn't,' said the dwarfie. 'You've heard tell of a country called Spain, maybe?'

'I have, seems so,' said Zach.

'Well then,' said Master Billy, 'the king of that country has a daughter, and that daughter is sick nigh to death. Now I have a bottle here in my pocket, and in the bottle is the medicine that will cure her. But it must be given her by a mortal man, and not by the likes of me. So do you take the bottle, and be off with you to Spain, and give the lady three drops from the bottle each morning for three days.'

'It's a longish way to go,' said Zach doubtfully.

84

'So 'tis,' said Master Billy. 'But I'll see you safe there and back again, and there's a bag of gold is the reward for curing her. There's been many a doctor trying his hand on that poor lady, but each one has left her worse than he found her. And the king, he's in *some* way about it all, and swears he'll have the head of the next one that comes with a cure that's no cure at all.'

'I'm not willing to lose my head for any lady,' said Zach.

The dwarfie made a fierce face at that. 'Am I telling you you're going to cure her, or am I not telling you?' said he.

Well, they talked a bit more, and in the end Zach agreed to go, for the little, small dwarfie of a boy that called himself Master Billy had a persuasive way with him; though Zach couldn't see what that dwarfie was going to get out of it for himself. However, Zach took the bottle and set out, and though the journey should have been a long one, it seemed a short one; and that must have been owing to Master Billy's magic.

So Zach came to Spain and called at the palace, and told the king he was come to cure his daughter.

'What!' said the king. 'Don't you know that all the doctors in the world have failed to cure her? And the next one that fails is to lose his head! Now go your ways home again, for I'm not willing to cut off your head, and that's a fact.'

But Zach said that if the lady would take his medicine she'd be ready to ride out hunting in three days' time; and he seemed so certain sure about it that at last the king said he might have a try. So Zach was taken up to the princess's room, and there she lay on the bed, flat on her back with her eyes shut, like as if she were dead.

Zach asked for a spoon, and he put the spoon between the princess's teeth, and dripped three drops from the bottle down her throat. And she opened her eyes and sat up.

'There now,' said Zach, 'what did I tell you?'

Next morning she was sitting up waiting for him. And when she had swallowed three more drops from the bottle, she rose from her bed and asked for some food.

On the third morning, when she had taken three more drops, she called to her waiting-women and bade them bring her riding habit, for she had a mind to go out hunting with the king.

You can fancy what rejoicing there was through all the kingdom of Spain. The king wanted to keep Zach with him as court physician, but Zach said no, he had a mind to go home. So home he went, carrying a great bag of gold with him.

And the first evening after he got back, as he was sitting by the fire, in came the little small dwarfie, Master Billy, wearing his red cap.

'Well, Zach,' said he, 'did your errand content you?'

'It did more than content me,' said Zach. 'And it's you I have to thank for it all.'

'Would you like to have another bag of gold as big as that one?' said Master Billy.

'Thank you all the same,' said Zach, 'but I don't know that I'm needing it.'

Master Billy made a fierce face again. 'And me by way of making you a rich man!' he said. 'Don't you be so stupid! Now hearken. There's a wrestling match up to Devonshire, with a bag of gold for the champion; and there's a great bragging bully of a man gives out that he can beat the whole world. But you shall beat him, Zach, for I shall be there to help you.'

Zach wasn't willing to go to Devonshire and wrestle with a big bully; to be sure he wasn't — *he* who had never wrestled in his life! But it seemed he had to do as that dwarfie told him. So to Devonshire he went. And when he got into the ring, and saw that great big bully dressed up in his wrestling-jacket, and looking down his nose at all the world, Zach's knees felt as if they'd turned to water. And when the bully gave him a shake of the hand before they began to wrestle, Zach thought for sure he'd broken every bone that was in his fingers, so fierce was that hand-grip. But then he looked down and saw Master Billy standing at his feet; and the next thing he knew, he had that great big bully fast by the shoulders of the jacket, and had lifted him over his head, and thrown him flat on his back on the turf in a fair fall. And that was the first round to Zach.

The crowd roared and cheered, and Zach and the big bully went at it again. Again Zach threw the bully over his head and laid him flat. And that was the second round to Zach. So it happened a third time. After that Zach was carried through the town by a shouting crowd who declared him to be the world's champion wrestler; and so at last he found himself

back home with another bag of gold, and feeling quite bewildered as to how it had all come about.

That evening, as he sat by the fire, came a knock at his door, and when he opened it, in skipped Master Billy.

'Evening to you, Zach,' said he, waving his red cap. 'Two bags of gold, and a third for the getting!'

'I'm rich enough already,' said Zach, 'and grateful I am to you for it.'

'Well then,' said Master Billy, 'would you be willing to do me a kindness?'

'I would so,' said Zach.

'This is the way of it,' said Master Billy. 'Me and my brothers are planning to pass over to Spain this night as ever is, to pay a visit to the king's daughter and bring her back with us. But 'tis you must persuade her to come, for the likes of us can't do it.'

'*Me* to persuade a lady!' said Zach.

'You will, soon as you take her by the hand,' said Master Billy. 'I'll see to that. So will you come?'

'I will,' said Zach, 'in return for your kindness.'

'But you must speak no work, good or bad, until I bid you,' said Master Billy, 'or else all our plans will come to naught.'

'Well then,' said Zach, 'I'll not speak a word.'

So the two of them went out of the door and across the lane and into a field. In the field there were hundreds of little dwarfies like Billy in red caps, and they were scampering about all over the place, and calling out 'Get me a horse! Get me a horse!' They were cutting down the ragworts that grew in the field and getting astride of them. As soon as each one got astride a ragwort, that ragwort turned into a little yellow horse and galloped away with its rider.

Zach was just about to call out, 'Get me a horse, too!' for he thought he mustn't be left behind. But he remembered in time that he wasn't to speak, and shut his mouth tight. Just then Master Billy came galloping up on a little yellow horse, and leading a yearling calf as white as milk.

'Here is *your* horse,' he said to Zach. 'So get you up, and off we'll go.'

Zach got up on the calf's back, and away they went, galloping, galloping, galloping, the whole company of them. Over fields and hedges and ditches they went, till they came to a great lake with an island in the middle of it. With one leap the little horses and their riders landed on the island; with another leap they leapt off the island and landed on the opposite shore. And with one leap the white calf, with Zach astride of him, was on that island, and with another leap he was on the opposite shore.

'My days!' cried Zach, before he could stop himself, 'that was *some* leap for a yearling calf!'

And no sooner had he said those words than something gave him a great blow on the head, and he tumbled off the calf, and lay senseless.

When he came to himself it was morning, and there he was, lying lonely by the lake, and no horses or riders or yearling calf to be seen anywhere. So he got up and walked round the lake, and made his way back home on foot, and weary he was before he reached his home.

Master Billy must have been angry, for he never came to visit Zach again; but he didn't steal away the bags of gold, so perhaps he wasn't so very angry after all.

And when Zach had sat by his fire and thought it all out, he decided that it was just as well he *had* spoken; for it wasn't likely that the king of Spain's daughter would have wanted to be brought away.

'Bless her little heart,' thought Zach. 'I reckon she's better off safe and sound in her father's palace, than going gallivanting round about the world with Master Billy and his kind!'

12. Monster Grabber and the King's Daughter

I   The Requiem

Once upon a time a young woodcutter, called Jonas, took his axe and went into the forest to chop down an oak tree. And on his way, what should he see but a fluffy-coated hare scampering along the path in front of him.

'Ah ha!' thought Jonas, 'that creature's coat would bring me in a pound or two if I sold it in the market.'

And he chased after the hare. He ran fast, but the hare ran faster. Could Jonas catch it? No, he couldn't. And the end of it was that he lost sight of the creature — and lost himself as well. He was in a part of the forest he had never been in before. He didn't know which way he should turn to get home; and to make matters worse, the sun had long set; under the forest trees it was dim, dim twilight, and soon it would be dark, dark night.

What to do? With night would come hungry animals, growling bears and prowling wolves, against whom a woodman's axe would be no sure defence. There was nothing for it but to climb up into a tree and spend the night among its branches. There he would be safe. So, finding an oak with convenient low-spreading branches, he climbed up into it; and resting his back against the trunk of the tree, he slept soundly until early morning.

He was awakened by a loud confusion of sounds beneath him: a roaring, a barking, a miaowing, a yelping, a screaming, a twittering, a squeaking. Cautiously he leaned from his branch and peered down. What did he see? Lying under the tree was the dead body of an elk, and gathered round it were many creatures, a lion, a cock, a bear, a horse, a greyhound, a lark, a wolf, a cat, an eagle, a fly, a rabbit, an ant, a fox, a sparrow and other creatures.

'It's mine to sing his requiem,' roared the lion. 'Was he not my life-long friend?'

'No, no, that's *my* privilege,' growled the bear. 'He was my children's dearly-loved playmate. He would take them all up on his back and trot with them here and there round and round among the trees for hours together.'

'But with me he ran races,' cried the horse, 'and if I won he was more pleased than if he won himself! Ah, how he would rub his cheek against my neck, and cry, "Well done, well done!" And shall I not now sing his praises and tell the world what a generous good-hearted fellow he was?'

'No one knew that better than I,' said the cat. 'One night when I was a kitten I lost myself in this forest, and I was oh so frightened and cold and miserable. But he lay down beside me and bade me cuddle up against his neck, and rubbed his soft cheek against me, and said, "Sleep, little one, you are safe with me. In the morning I will show you the way home." '

Then the eagle said scornfully, 'You with your roaring, growling, howling, squealing miaowling voices! *I* have a lordly voice fit to sing the requiem of a lord.'

Then said the fly, 'But you would only have a single voice, *I* can bring a hundred voices!'

But the ant said, 'Be bothered with your buzzing!' Then he looked up into the tree and saw Jonas. 'See!' he cried. 'See friends, here is someone who can come and settle our dispute, and decide who shall sing and who shall not sing.'

Then all the creatures called out to Jonas to come down, and of course he had to come. He climbed down, he considered for a while, then he said, 'What can I say to you? I myself must sing. Otherwise we shall never get your friend under the earth. But you must all join in the chorus.'

'That is fair, that is something *like* a decision!' cried all the creatures, 'and of course we will all join in the chorus!'

Then Jonas began to sing, and the song went like this:

Jonas	'Alas, alas, our friend lies dead,'
All the creatures	'Ah, lies dead!'
Jonas	'To Paradise his soul has fled,'
All the creatures	'His soul has fled.'
Jonas	'There in Heaven's green fields we pray His soul may graze till Judgement day.'
All the creatures	'Till Judgement day.'
Jonas	'Then his loving friends to greet With joyful songs, and laughter sweet.'
All the creatures	'And laughter sweet.'

The creatures all agreed that this was a beautiful requiem.

The eagle said, 'A grand song, a lovely song!'

The cat said, 'It was so lovely that it made me cry.'

The lark said, 'I will sing it over and over again up in the blue sky. All the bright sunbeams and the little white clouds will gather round to listen.'

The bear said, 'I shall teach it to my cubs.'

The wolf said, 'I shall hum it over to myself as I prowl through the forest.'

The horse said, 'We shall none of us ever forget it.'

The lion said, 'Now we must reward the singer. Each of us must give him our strength. He has only to call out the name of one of us and turn a somersault, and at once he will take on the form of a lion, or a fly, or a horse, or a cat, or an ant, or of any other creature he wishes.'

Jonas couldn't quite see how being able to turn himself into such little creatures as a fly or an ant could be of any use to him, or how in the course of his quiet and orderly life he should ever need to turn himself into such a fierce creature as a lion. However, since the gifts were offered in gratitude, he received them gratefully. And having thanked the creatures again and again, he left them to spread the turf over the body of their dead friend, and went on his way.

II   Monster Grabber

At the edge of the forest Jonas met the king's swineherd. The poor lad was weeping bitterly.

'What's the matter, my boy?' said Jonas.

'Matter enough!' cried the boy. 'That wicked Monster Grabber is going to eat all my pigs!'

'What are you saying?' said Jonas. 'How has Monster Grabber got you into his power?'

'Well, it's not my fault,' wailed the boy. 'The king himself is to blame. The king lost himself in the forest a few days ago. He couldn't find his way out. But from who knows where, Monster Grabber appeared and offered to show the king the way out of the forest – but only if the king would promise to give Monster Grabber each day a pig, and when there were no more pigs left, the king must give the monster his daughter, his only child. Now,' said the boy, 'the king has said that he will give his daughter to wife to anyone who can get the better of Monster Grabber.'

'Splendid!' said Jonas. 'We must try and lay hands on this pig-eater. Cheer up! I myself am just cut out to be the king's son-in-law. So don't worry any more.'

Then Jonas went to the king and spoke his mind. The king agreed that Jonas should herd the pigs with the swineherd.

So Jonas herded the pigs the first day. As he and the swineherd were driving them home in the evening, Monster Grabber suddenly appeared, seized a pig and made off with it into the forest. But Jonas called out the name of the horse, turned a somersault, and became a horse. The horse, galloping very fast, made a big loop, got ahead of the monster, and turned back to meet him face to face.

'Good evening, Monster Grabber,' said the horse.

'Good evening, horse,' said the monster.

'What are you doing here with that stupid pig?' said the horse. 'Don't you know that in the north sea pirates are attacking a ship? The sailors are bravely defending themselves, and if you don't hurry to help the pirates, the sailors are going to beat them off.'

'Dear little horse!' said the monster. 'Is this really true? Then I must hurry! Hold this pig for me, little brother. I'll be back directly.'

93

So saying Monster Grabber rushed away. The horse changed back into Jonas, and Jonas drove the pig home to the swineherd.

Next day toward evening came the monster, quite peevish, bustling along, seized a pig again and carried it off. But Jonas called out the name of the eagle, turned a somersault, became an eagle, flew in a loop to meet the monster, and asked in astonishment, 'Are you eating pig's meat today?'

'What else is there to eat, little Father Eagle?' said the monster. 'How many times have we poor monsters had to chew on rope and string from hunger, and even swallowed bits of iron and nails.'

'How can you be so simple?' said the eagle. 'Over there beyond the forest robbers are stealing the rich farmer's butter and cheese. The farmer and his men are beating them off with pitchforks – if you hurry you can get plenty of cheese, and help the robbers too.'

'What! Is this really true?' cried the monster. 'Well then, little Father Eagle, be so kind as to look after this pig for me, and I'll get my share of the spoil!' And he rushed away.

Then of course the eagle turned back into Jonas, drove the pig to the swineherd, and went laughing home.

On the third day Jonas herded the pigs without the monster appearing, and already evening stood before the door. So Jonas drove his pigs home to the sty, and he thought, 'I suppose now that good-for-nothing Monster Grabber will come in the night. I shall have to stay on the perch in the henroost as a cock, and wait for him.' So Jonas called out 'Cock!', turned a somersault, became a cock, and sat on the perch in the henroost.

Sure enough at midnight arrived Monster Grabber, quite starving, and set about the door of the pigsty. But immediately the cock Jonas began to crow, and at that sound the monster fled away without a pig.

But do you think that such a scoundrel would run off empty handed? Not a bit of it! As he came past the king's palace, Monster Grabber snatched the king's daughter out of bed and carried her off.

'The devil take you!' said the king to Jonas next morning. 'A fine guard you are. Better you'd let Monster Grabber have the pigs, than allow him to carry off my daughter!'

'No need to speak like that, little Father,' said Jonas. 'You just leave it to me.'

94

III   The King's Daughter

Now you must know that Monster Grabber lived in a golden palace inside a mountain. When he wanted to get into his palace he struck the mountain with his fist and it opened to let him in, and closed again behind him.

So Jonas changed himself into a greyhound, and ran swiftly to the mountain. Then, changing into Jonas, he struck the mountain with his fist. But would it open for him? No, it would not! What to do?

He changed himself into a lark and flew right up to the very top of the mountain. There he searched around and found a little tiny hole. So he changed himself into an ant, sat astride a grain of sand, and slid down through the hole into the depths of the mountain. When he got to the bottom sure enough there was the golden palace with the king's daughter sitting at a window. Poor girl, she was weeping bitterly.

So Jonas, changing himself into his own shape, called up to her, 'Dear princess, no need to weep, I have come to take you home!'

But the princess cried out, 'Ah, ah, how did you get here? You must go away quickly! If the monster comes he will tear you to pieces!'

And sure enough at that moment the monster appeared and, howling with rage, fell upon Jonas. But Jonas changed himself into a lion, and attacked the monster with teeth and claws. Heh! but that was a fight. For hours they fought but neither could get the better of the other. So at last Lion Jonas somersaulted head over heels, became a fly, and sat on the monster's head to rest and think awhile. What was he to do? Ah of course, he must call the animals to his aid.

'Lion!' shrilled the fly, 'Eagle, greyhound, horse, wolf, bear, cat, fox, rabbit, sparrow, ant, lark, cock, to my aid – to my aid!' And immediately they all came and rushed upon the monster, the larger animals biting and tearing, the smaller ones nipping and buzzing, rushing up his nose and blinding his eyes – until at last there was the wretched monster howling for mercy.

'Do you deserve mercy?' said the lion. 'You who have had no mercy on anyone. What do you say, animals, shall we spare him or not?'

'I think,' said the horse, 'that we should spare him, if he will take himself off to the end of the world and never more come back.'

'And to make matters more sure,' said the sparrow, 'let us first change him into a harmless moth.'

'Oh yes,' cried all the animals, 'let us do that!' And they all began to shout:

> *'Monster Grabber, hear us say,*
> *A moth you shall be from this day,*
> *And to the world's end fly away.'*

With a despairing howl, Monster Grabber vanished, the side of the mountain opened, and in triumphal procession all the creatures escorted Jonas and the princess back to the king's palace. And then to be sure Jonas married the princess.

And as to the wedding feast, there has been nothing to equal it since the world began, because all the creatures were at the feast, and of course all the king's people came as well. Who had a horse came riding, who had no horse came walking, and those who could neither ride nor walk came in carriages, carts, and wheelbarrows, but no one missed that wedding feast, come as they might.

13. The New Horse

Once upon a time a farmer went to market and bought a black horse. It was a splendid animal, and the farmer had to pay a big sum of money for it. But he rode it home well content, finding it docile and very intelligent.

'There, my beauty,' says he, leading the horse into the stable, bedding it down, and giving it a feed of corn.

'Wu-uff, wuff, wuff,' said the horse, rubbing his soft nose against the farmer's hand.

'Ah,' said the farmer, 'I see you and I are going to get on well together.'

And he shut the stable-door, and went away into the farm kitchen to get his supper.

Next morning, the farmer, the farmer's wife, the farmer's three sons, and Mr Skild, the farmer's neighbour, all went to the stable to have a look at the new horse. And all were loud in their praises of that horse.

'I won't work him today,' said the farmer. 'There's nothing special I want done at the moment. So I'll give him time to accustom himself to us.'

'*Wuff, wuff, wuff,*' said the horse.

And there he was, nibbling the farmer's fingers with his soft lips, as much as to say, 'I like you. I do like you!'

But what was the farmer's astonishment when next moment the horse gave a loud whinny, flung up his heels, leaped over the half-door of the stable, and galloped away into a nearby forest.

The farmer, the farmer's three sons, the stable-boy, and the farmer's neighbour, Mr Skild, all pelted after the horse. And there on a grass plat under the trees, they saw him galloping round in circles, galloping, galloping till the sweat ran off him.

Not one of the men could stop him, not one of them could catch him: when they tried to lay hands on him, he kicked and reared and plunged. And round the grass plat he went, and round and round at that mad gallop: until, all of a sudden, he brought up with a jerk, and stood with his head hanging, and trembling in every limb.

Then the farmer took him by the forelock, and led him back to the stable.

'If I were you,' said Mr Skild, the farmer's neighbour, 'I'd sell him quick. For sure as I'm alive the animal's bewitched.'

'Then how could I sell him?' said the farmer, who was an honest fellow.

'Well, put a bullet through his head, and have done,' said Mr Skild.

'I'll do no such thing!' said the farmer. 'It would break my heart.'

Mr Skild shrugged his shoulders and went away. The horse was standing with his head drooped; and he was streaming with sweat. The farmer took a cloth and a brush, and he and the stable-boy gave the poor animal a good grooming. And the horse said, '*Wuff, wuff, wuff,*' and rubbed his head against the farmer's arm.

'I'm sure I don't know what to make of you,' said the farmer. 'But I think we best leave you quiet for the day.' So, bidding the stable-boy fill the water bucket, he put a good feed of oats in the manger, and an armful of hay in the rack, he then went out, taking the stable-boy with him and locking the stable-door behind them.

'Master,' said the boy, 'there's witches in the forest.'

'And what's that got to do with anything?' said the farmer.

'Dunno,' said the boy. 'Thought it might have.'

Last thing that evening the farmer took a lantern and went to the stable. The horse was lying down and sleeping quietly. The farmer gave a sigh of relief and went to his bed. But he didn't sleep well, he was having nightmares in which the horse seemed to be galloping round in circles on the ceiling. It was a relief when next morning he found the horse quiet in the stable, and greeting him with a friendly '*Wuff, wuff, wuff!*' So, after breakfast, he led the horse out into a field that he intended to sow with corn. And he harnessed the horse to the plough.

'*Yip, yip, yip,* my beauty!' said he.

Up and down, up and down across the field went the horse, willing as willing, and the green grass turning into brown furrows behind the plough, and the air full of the flapping of white wings, as a flock of gulls came wheeling and screaming to pick the worms from the turned-up earth.

So all went smoothly until noon. And then suddenly the horse seemed to go mad. He kicked over the traces, flung up his head, gave a loud whinny, and off at a gallop to the forest, with a broken trace dangling about him, and the farmer chasing after him, shouting and panting.

But of course the farmer couldn't keep up with a galloping horse: and when he reached the clearing in the forest, there was the horse galloping round and round in a crazy circle till the sweat ran off him, and foam flew from his nostrils, and his eyes seemed to be starting from his head. And then, all of a sudden, he brought up with a jerk, and stood with his head hanging, and trembling in every limb.

And the farmer, almost scared out of his wits, took the shuddering animal by the forelock and led him home.

'I don't know what to do!' said the farmer, nigh sobbing with bewilderment.

'Master,' said the stable-boy, 'it's them witches as is at the bottom of this.'

'Witches!' said the farmer, 'I doubt if there are such things.'

'Oh, but there are,' said the stable-boy. 'And if you'll let me ride the horse tomorrow, I'll prove it to you.'

Well, at first the farmer wasn't willing to let the boy ride the horse, fearing some harm might come to the lad. But the boy kept on pestering until he got his way. So next morning, just before noon, there was the horse saddled and bridled, with the boy up on his back, trotting sedately along the path to the forest. The sun was shining, the birds were singing, everything was as pretty and peaceful as could be: until just at the entrance to the forest, the boy heard a shrill cry of '*Hup! hup! hup!*' And see – there perched on the horse in front of him was a hideous old woman.

'*Hup! hup! hup!*' shrilled the hideous old woman, kicking with her bony heels, and slapping with her skinny wrinkled hands.

'*Hup! hup! hup!*' The horse began to sweat, the horse began to gallop. He came to the clearing, and now he was galloping madly round and round with the hideous old woman kicking with her bony heels, and slapping with one of her bony hands, whilst with the other she was trying to snatch the reins away from the boy.

'Oh no you don't!' shouted the boy, clinging on to the reins with all his might. But he couldn't pull up the horse; the horse was still galloping round and round, and nothing the boy could do would stop him. The boy tried to push the old woman off the horse. Could he budge her? No, he couldn't. But he still had the reins, and he wasn't letting go of them. And all at once he knew what to do.

Stooping low, and with a violent tug at the right-hand rein, he drove the horse up against the overhanging branches of a holly tree. A prickly branch caught in the old woman's hair, and as the horse galloped on, there she was, lifted off the horse's back, hanging by her hair in the tree, and screaming till the whole wood echoed.

It was easy now for the boy to pull up the horse, and he turned and rode back to the holly tree.

'Let me down!' screamed the old woman.

'Not I!' said the boy.

'Oh, oh, oh!' screamed the old woman. 'Help me down, and I'll give you a purse full of gold!'

'I don't want your gold, you wicked old witch,' said the boy. 'I wouldn't touch it for a kingdom.'

'Then what *do* you want?' screamed the old woman.

'I want a promise from you,' said the boy.

'Shan't give it you!' screamed the old woman.

'Then you can hang there till doomsday,' said the boy.

He turned the horse, and was riding off, when the old woman screamed again.

'Eh! What is it you want me to promise?'

'Never to ride the horse again,' said the boy.

'Shan't promise no such thing,' screamed the old woman.

'Then hang there and rot,' said the boy. 'I'm going home'.

The old woman screamed, the old woman struggled; but all she did was to get herself more tangled up in the holly tree. The boy was riding away now; but very, very slowly. He was chuckling to himself.

'Stop, stop, *stop*!' screamed the old woman.

The boy pulled up the horse.

'Come back!' screamed the old woman.

The boy rode back. 'Well?' he said.

'What was it you wanted me to promise?' said the old woman.

'Never to ride my master's horse again,' said the boy. 'And whilst

you're about it, you might promise never to come within a hundred miles of my master's farm. For neighbours such as you aren't healthy, and that's a fact.'

'I *hate* your master and I hate *you*!' screamed the old woman. 'Oh, how I hate you!'

'That's no odds,' said the boy, 'so long as you leave us in peace. Come now, be sensible! Sign this piece of paper with your promise and let us each go our own way.'

'I haven't got a pen,' said the witch.

'Here you are,' said the boy reaching behind his ear and holding out his hand.

With an evil snarl the witch snatched the pen and scrawled her name on the paper.

The boy pulled out his knife, reached up and cut her down.

Quivering with rage the witch kicked the ground with her heel. And as she kicked, so the ground opened into a gaping hole. The old woman slid down into the hole. The ground closed over her.

And the boy rode home on his master's horse, which from that day onward, was a model of all that a horse should be.

14. The Beauty of the Golden Star

A merchant and his wife had an only son, called Alfin – a brave, good, handsome lad, none better. And when Alfin was but just grown-up, he had a wonderful dream. In this dream he saw a most beautiful maiden who leaned from a window of a diamond castle, held out her arms to him and said, 'I am the Beauty of the Golden Star, kept captive by a monstrous dragon. Oh, Alfin, will you not pity me, will you not rescue me? Come to me, Alfin, come, come!'

So next morning Alfin said to his parents, 'My dear father, my darling mother, now I must leave you. I cannot tell how long it will be before I see you again. So give me your blessings. I am setting out to seek the Beauty of the Golden Star: to fight and kill the dragon that holds her captive, or die in the attempt.'

Well, to be sure, Alfin's father said it was all foolishness; and Alfin's mother wept, and begged Alfin not to leave them. But Alfin was determined to go. So, with his sword at his belt, and mounted on a good horse, go he did.

He rode, rode, rode. He rode for hundreds of miles, asking every one he met where he could find the Beauty of the Golden Star. But no one could tell him. Some people said that there was not, and never had been, any such person. Others said oh yes, there had been such a person, but she had died long ago. And yet others, to tease him, told him that he would find her at the next cross-roads, seated in a golden coach, and waiting for him. Then he would gallop on in high hopes: only to find, when he reached the cross-roads, a thief hanging from a gibbet, or a scarecrow set up to frighten away the birds. And on he rode, and on.

After a while, he was going through a great forest. At first the road through the forest was wide and plain to see; but as he went on the road became narrower and narrower, until it was a mere path: and the sun had gone down behind the trees, and soon it would be night. So, coming to a grassy clearing, Alfin dismounted, left his horse to graze where it would, knowing that the good animal would never desert him: whilst he himself sat down under a tree to wait for morning. He was tired, but no, he couldn't sleep: his mind was too full of thoughts about the Beauty of the Golden Star, and the vision of her as she had appeared to him in his dream. 'Come to me Alfin, come, come!' Surely she was calling to him still!

It was getting on for midnight when he heard far off a sound of music, and saw away among the trees a glimmer of light. And as he listened and watched, the sound of music grew louder, and the light became brighter. Under the darkness of the trees the light was moving towards him, glancing here upon a tree trunk, there upon a bush, or upon the ruts in the winding path at the foot of the trees: until, suddenly, that light was blazing in his eyes – and behold, dancing towards him came seven most beautiful fairies, clothed in rainbow-coloured garments that seemed to float about them, as they formed a circle round the tree under which he sat, and joining hands began to dance and sing. And still the music sounded in his ears, though where it came from he couldn't tell; nor could he understand one word of the fairies' song: all he knew was that it was so beautiful, so beautiful, that it filled his heart with joy, and yet he felt like weeping.

So for a long time, or a short time, he knew not which (for indeed he had lost all sense of time) the seven fairies danced and sang, whilst he watched and listened spellbound, until suddenly the music stopped, and the dancing feet were still, the fairies unlinked their hands, and stood for a moment without sound or motion. And then one of them – perhaps the most lovely of them all – came to stand at Alfin's feet, and said in a voice that was like the cooing of a dove, 'Alfin, whither you are bound we know, and we would help you if we may. But have you considered the terrible perils that await you?'

'I have considered nothing,' said Alfin. 'All I know is that I must either find, and win for my bride, the Beauty of the Golden Star, or perish in the attempt.'

The fairy laughed. 'No, no, Alfin, we would not have you perish. I have here a little gift that may help you in time of need.'

And she put something into his hand.

What was that something? Just a walnut!

Alfin didn't think that a walnut would be much help to him, but he thanked the fairy politely. And then the other fairies clustered round him, crying out, 'He must have more than one nut!' And they gave him two more walnuts. And then, laughing and singing, they joined hands and rose into the air, up and up.

The light of their going became less and less, until it dwindled away among the clouds: all was darkness.

And Alfin fell asleep.

The rays of the rising sun, shining through the trees, woke him in the morning. And, having eaten some of the bread and cheese which he carried in his wallet, he called his faithful horse. 'Greco, Greco, Greco!' he called, for that was the horse's name. With an answering whinny Greco came trotting towards him from among the trees. And Alfin jumped on to Greco's back, and rode on through the forest, and out of the forest.

He had no idea which way he should go: he just rode straight on. By and by he saw in the distance the blazing of a fire, and galloping towards that blaze, came to where an old man stood by the side of the road, stirring with an iron fork something in a cauldron that hung over a fire of brushwood. The old man had a long white beard that reached to his feet, his face was thin and haggard, and his ragged tunic was of a fashion that surely had never been seen on earth within the memory of man.

'Oh good old man,' cried Alfin, jumping off Greco's back, 'what is it you are stirring in that cauldron? And why are you stirring — you who look so tired?'

'I stir, I stir,' answered the old man, looking up at Alfin with smoke-bleared eyes. 'For three thousand years - ah, alas for my sins! — I have been condemned to stand here stirring, *turutun, turutun, turutun*. In this cauldron are gathered together all the virtues and vices of mankind. But the virtues, being solid, lie at the bottom, and the vices, being light, rise to the top. See, my son, how they rise — these bubble vices of many colours, black, red, green, yellow, purple — they rise, they float, they fly

away and burst to shower down mischief all over the world. But the golden virtues – ah, with all my stirring I can raise but few of them; it seems they have no wish to visit the haunts of evil men, and seldom, oh so seldom, does one leave the cauldron. They huddle there together at the bottom of the cauldron, as you see; and I must stir, and stir, and *stir* to rouse them into activity. It seems I must go on stirring until the end of time. And, oh how weary I am, how weary!'

'Give me your fork,' said Alfin. 'I will stir a while, and you shall rest.'

'Oh how kind!' said the old man.

And handing the fork to Alfin, he lay down beside the cauldron, and immediately fell asleep.

Turutun, turutun, turutun. Alfin stirred without ceasing. And lo, as he stirred, several of the golden virtues rose up from the bottom of the

107

cauldron, hovered uncertainly for a moment over the cauldron's top, and then floated away over the land, some in one direction, some in another. And Alfin laughed and said, 'Good luck to you, my little virtues, a prosperous journey to you, little virtues! And may the troubled hearts of men receive you kindly!'

All through that day, and all through the following night, Alfin stayed by the old man's side, and stirred the cauldron whilst the old man slept. But when the sun rose on the second morning, Alfin thought again of the Beauty of the Golden Star; and he gave the old man a gentle prod which roused him into wakefulness.

'Now I must leave you, old fellow,' he said, 'because I have to find the Beauty of the Golden Star. It is to find her that I have left my home, and find her I must and will.'

The old man flung his skinny arms round Alfin and said, 'Oh how grateful I am, how grateful! After three thousand years of wakefulness you have given me the blessing of sleep! And now refreshed I can take up my task again with a light heart. Here is a parting gift for you!'

And he plucked a hair from his beard. 'Keep it carefully,' he said, putting the hair into Alfin's hand. 'It will help you, dear lad. Yes, it will help you in the hour of your need.'

Alfin didn't think that the hair could be of any help to him, whether now, or at any other time; but he thanked the old man politely, put the hair away in his wallet, and jumped on to the back of his faithful Greco, who had all this time been waiting near him, at times dozing, at times cropping the wayside grass.

'One last word,' said the old man. 'At the end of this road there are seven overflowing river torrents, and beyond the river torrents there are seven mountains, and beyond the seven mountains there are seven forests. It is not until you have passed the rivers, the mountains and the forests that you will find the Beauty of the Golden Star. But be of good cheer, Alfin my lad; there is an old saying that "Love shall still be lord of all", and so it shall prove to be to the one who is stout of heart.'

'Oh, I don't doubt it!' laughed Alfin.

And he rode away: rivers, mountains, forests – what were they to him? But signposts pointing to his goal – the dwelling of the Beauty of the Golden Star.

So he came to the end of the road; and there before him now were the seven river torrents: a foaming, fast rushing mass of waters, beyond which rose the steep sides of a seemingly endless range of mountains.

'Now Greco, we must prove our mettle!' said Alfin.

And he urged the horse into the foaming waters.

Greco can find no bottom for his feet. He is swimming gallantly, but the foaming waters are rising above his head. He is pushed this way and that by the waves: now all but the tip of his nostrils is under water – surely he is drowning, and surely Alfin will drown with him!

No, no, *no*! Alfin remembers the gift of the fairies – the walnuts they had given him 'to help him in time of need', as they had said. Now surely the time of need has come! He takes a nut from his pocket, cracks it open with his teeth, and flings it into the swirling torrent. What happens? Up out of the water, immediately under Greco's feet, rises a golden bridge. And Greco gallops across the bridge, and arrives safely on the other side of the river torrents.

Hurrah! One difficulty overcome! But now Alfin must cross the seven mountains whose tops are hidden in the clouds, and whose sides rise sheer out of the ground, straight, steep, without path or foothold. Alfin sets Greco at the first of these mountains. Greco is willing enough, but Alfin might as well set the poor animal at a pane of glass. And for every step the horse takes forward, he slides back two. No, there is no climbing that mountain!

Then Alfin thinks again of the nuts the fairies had given him. He has still two left. He cracks one, takes out the kernel, and gives it to Greco. Greco swallows it down – and see! Now he is going up that mountain as easily as if he were walking in a meadow. And when he gets to the top of that first mountain what does Greco do? He takes a leap and lands on the top of the second mountain, and with yet another leap lands on the top of the third mountain.

And so he leaps from mountain top to mountain top, until he lands on the summit of the seventh. My word, that was a powerful nut, and no mistake! Alfin is laughing, and blessing those fairies from his heart.

Now looking down from the top of this seventh mountain, Alfin can see the seven forests that he must pass through before he reaches that blessed country where he will find the Beauty of the Golden Star. Oh, he does not doubt that he will reach her! And cautiously, cautiously, he guides his willing Greco down the mountain-side, among great boulders and jagged rocks: and reaching the bottom, he enters the first of the seven forests, and pushes on under the dark crowding branches of the trees.

But what a forest! Thickets this way, thickets that way, great logs lying across the path, and every now and then the path ending in a precipice, and Greco pulling up with a jerk, just on the edge of it, and Alfin having to turn back and find another path. And now – hark! What is that noise behind him, a loud howling that draws ever nearer and nearer, the howling of a pack of wolves! The wolves come rushing out from under the trees on all sides of him. Alfin sets Greco off galloping, the wolves chase after him, they are leaping at Alfin's legs, they chase him from one forest into another forest, and into another forest, and yet another, they chase him into the seventh forest – what to do, oh what to do? Alfin takes the third nut out of his wallet, cracks it and flings it down among the wolves . . . . And all in a moment the wolves vanish.

And Alfin comes to the end of the seventh forest, and out into a wide, grassy plain, where red poppies nod amongst the grass, and roses white and pink scent the air on either side of a smooth path that stretches on and on across the plain. There in the distance, rise the gleaming walls of a beautiful palace – the palace, surely, of the Beauty of the Golden Star!

Alfin gives a shout of triumph. 'Ah, my good horse, Greco, see, see, the end of all our journeying! Speed on, speed on! Soon you shall rest!'

Greco sets off at a demure trot: no, he will not gallop, however eagerly Alfin urges him. Greco is turning his head uneasily, this way and that way. And well may he turn his head, and well may he be uneasy – for suddenly, rushing across the plain towards them comes a monstrous Dragon. 'Be off!' roars the Dragon, hurling himself on Alfin. 'What business have you here? This is *my* kingdom, *mine*! I allow no trespassers!'

Alfin draws his sword, he slashes at the Dragon: the Dragon turns into a crocodile, Alfin slashes at the crocodile: the crocodile turns into a toad, Alfin leaps from the saddle, and with one blow of his sword – off goes the toad's head.

'So perish all who would come between me and the Beauty of the Golden Star!' cries Alfin.

And he gallops on.

Now he is drawing nearer and ever nearer to the gleaming walls of the palace; now he has reached the palace gates; now he sets his willing Greco at a leap, now he is over the gates; now he is galloping up through the courtyard of the palace – there is no one to stop him. Now he has reached the great entrance door of the palace – and see! There looking out of an open window is the Beauty of the Golden Star. She is dressed in a snow-white robe, and on her forehead, just where her hair parts to fall in golden tresses on either side of her lovely face, shines a star so brilliant that Alfin is almost blinded by the sight of it.

'Ah, my deliverer, you have come at last!' she cries. And she hurries to fling open the great entrance door of the palace.

Now Alfin has leaped off Greco's back; now he is inside the palace; now he and the Beauty of the Golden Star are in each other's arms . . . . . But the moment after that – hark! A screaming and a trampling, and a *thud, thud, thud,* that sets the floors of the palace shaking, and the walls shuddering! Who comes? It is the Mother Dragon in a frenzy of rage, come to avenge the death of her son.

The Beauty of the Golden Star quickly pushes Alfin into a little room, slams the door on him, and stands outside the door with her back against it, facing the furious Mother Dragon. 'Ah, Mamma Dragon,' says she, 'what is the matter? Has some one hurt you, or are you ill, that you complain so bitterly?'

The Mamma Dragon thrusts the Beauty of the Golden Star out of her way. With a butt of her head she breaks down the door of the little room where Alfin is hiding. Alfin is ready with his sword, but the Mamma Dragon turns into an ant. Alfin puts out his foot to stamp upon the ant: the ant turns into a vulture and flies up screaming. Alfin makes a cut at the vulture with his sword: the vulture turns into a lovely girl. Alfin's sword dangles loosely in his hand – how can he wound a lovely girl? But the Beauty of the Golden Star gives the lovely girl a slap: the lovely girl turns into a hideous old witch. The old witch screams out a curse upon the Beauty of the Golden Star, but before she has half uttered it, Alfin swings his sword and cuts off her head.

'Alfin, Alfin,' cries the Beauty of the Golden Star, 'you have slain the Dragon, you have slain the Mother Dragon. I thank you from my heart. Now I have no more enemies to fear. Here in my palace I can live in peace.'

'Oh no, not here,' says Alfin. 'My good horse, Greco, shall carry us both home. And in my parents' house we will hold our wedding.'

'Alfin,' said the Beauty of the Golden Star, 'I think you forget yourself. Go home with *you*, marry *you*! Who are *you* that you should so presume? A mere merchant's son! Pray does a mere merchant's son consider himself a match for the Beauty of the Golden Star? What impudence! But there – I forgive you, because you have saved my life.'

Alfin is astounded, he can hardly believe his ears. His heart is filled with bitterness and injured pride. 'As I journeyed hither,' he says, 'I came across an old man stirring a cauldron. From that cauldron rose many coloured bubbles. The old man told me that these bubbles were the vices of the world. Did one bubble happen to fly this way? And was it the bubble of pride? And did it perchance come to find rest in the heart of the Beauty of the Golden Star? When I parted from the old man he gave me a hair from his beard. He said it would help me in the hour of my need. But I have no more need of help, all hours are henceforth alike to me. And so as a parting gift – take this hair. And may you sometimes think not unkindly of the foolish young fellow whose heart you have broken.'

And he turned and strode away out of the diamond palace.

'Alfin! Alfin!' A voice calling him. Light footsteps hurrying after him. Whose voice, whose footsteps? The Beauty of the Golden Star's. She catches Alfin by the arm, she looks up into his face, there are tears in her eyes, but she is smiling.

'Dear Alfin, forgive my cruel words. It was not my heart that uttered them. It was the curse that the old witch laid upon me just before you killed her. But the old man's blessed gift has vanquished that curse. And so, Alfin, forget it! Alfin, dear Alfin, take me home.'

Who so happy now as Alfin? He lifts the Beauty of the Golden Star on to the back of his faithful Greco. He jumps up himself. Away they go. And if the journey is a long one, it is also a happy one. They meet no wolves in the seven forests. The fairies' nuts have not lost their virtue, and by their virtue the seven mountains are easily scaled. When they come to the seven torrents, there is the golden bridge still standing for them to gallop across. But when they come to the place where the old man had been standing under the hedge stirring the cauldron, no old man do they see. They see only the cauldron, lying upside down on the grass.

'I think an angel must have come and carried the old man up to heaven,' says Alfin as they gallop past.

And truly that is what has happened. For the old man's time of penance is over.

And so on they go, and come into the fairies' wood, and there are the fairies flying round them, and singing, 'Well done, Alfin! A welcome home awaits you, Alfin! Now you and your bride shall live in happiness ever after!'

And so they did.

15. How Jack Made His Fortune

A young boy called Jack lived with his father and mother on a farm up above the moors. Of course Jack went to school, but the school was in a village some way from the moors, too far for Jack to come home for dinner. So, every day, Jack's mother packed him up some sandwiches. She also gave him three pennies that he might buy himself a glass of milk or some ginger beer or anything else he fancied at the village shop.

Oh, and I mustn't forget to tell you that Jack was a favourite at the school because he had a pan pipe on which he could play very skilfully. The other children liked to dance to it, and sometimes even the schoolmaster himself would join in the fun.

Well now, our story begins on a May morning, with Jack on his way to school as usual. On his way he had to go through a wood. A stream flowed through the wood, and at one spot the stream widened out into a pool bordered with small bushes. Jack had just passed this pool when he met some big boys. One of the boys was carrying a little kitten. He was dangling the poor little thing by the scruff of its neck and swinging it this way and that as he walked.

'Oh,' said Jack, 'what are you going to do with that poor little kitten?'

'Do with it,' laughed the boy, 'why drown it of course!'

'Oh, no, please,' said Jack, 'please, please don't do that! Let me have it! I'll give you three pence for it.'

'Three pennies ain't much,' said the boy.

'But it's all I have,' said Jack.

'Oh, all right,' said the boy.

So Jack gave the boy his three pennies, and the boy gave him the kitten. Then the boy and his two companions went off laughing.

'I shall take you home,' said Jack to the kitten, 'but first I have to go to school. Do you think you could curl up here under this hawthorn bush until I come back?'

The kitten thought she could. And she purred with delight when Jack gave her his little packet of sandwiches, for she was very hungry.

That day Jack was very hungry too. He had to go without anything to eat, he couldn't even buy himself a glass of milk because he had given away his pennies. Never mind, he had saved the kitten's life, and that consoled him. And after school, you may be sure, he was all in a hurry to get back to the hawthorn bush. But before he reached it, he met those big boys again, and this time it was a puppy they were dragging along by a cord tied round its neck.

'Oh,' said Jack, 'don't, don't, you're hurting it! Where are you taking it?'

'Where?' laughed the biggest boy. 'To the pool to drown it . . . Unless of course you've any more pennies to spare.'

'You know I haven't!' cried Jack. 'You know I haven't!'

'Then give's your coat,' said the boy. '*And* your cap.'

So Jack took off his coat and his cap and gave them to the boy, and the boy gave Jack the puppy. And the boy and his two companions went off laughing.

'I expect you're hungry, my puppy?' said Jack.

'Yes, I am,' whimpered the puppy.

'And I haven't anything for you to eat,' said Jack. 'Never mind, you shall have a good meal when we get home. You shall have a playmate too.'

And he took the puppy to the hawthorn bush, where they found the kitten curled up fast asleep.

'Wake up kitty, we're going home!' cried Jack.

So, carrying the kitten, and with the puppy trotting at his heels, Jack went home.

But when his mother saw him coming in without his cap and coat, and with the kitten in his arms and the puppy at his heels, she cried out, 'Oh Jack, whatever *have* you been doing?'

So Jack told her all about it, and she said, 'I really don't know what to do about you. There's only your shabby old play coat for you to go to school in tomorrow and if *you* don't mind your going to school in it, I do!

It'll put me to shame! And you'd better get rid of those little animals before your Dad comes home, if you don't want a strapping.'

'Get rid of them?' said Jack. 'And let those horrid boys catch them again and drown them! I shall do no such thing!'

And he took them up to his bedroom, and coaxed his mother, who was really very kind-hearted, into giving them both a good meal.

That night the puppy slept at the end of Jack's bed, and the kitten slept curled up in Jack's arms. But in the morning, when Jack's father saw them, he said, 'Haven't we enough cats about the place already, but you must needs bring us another? And as for that pup – *he'll* never make a sheep dog, I can tell by the looks of him. So just you take them both back to where you found them, my lad, or it'll be the worse for you.'

That morning Jack set out for school with a heavy heart. Kitten and Puppy were trotting along beside him, happy as could be. 'See how they trust me,' said Jack to himself, 'how can I get rid of them, how *can* I?'

When he got into the wood he sat down by the pool to think things over. He felt very, very unhappy. And Puppy rubbed his little nose against Jack's knee and said, 'What's the matter Jack – why aren't you happy?'

So Jack told him. 'And I daren't take you home again!' he said. 'It isn't so much that I should mind a strapping, but I *know* my Dad will turn you out of doors.'

'Then why *go* home?' croaked a voice. And out of the pool jumped a young frog.

'What else can I do?' said Jack. 'If I don't go home, we shall all starve.'

'Oh no you won't,' said the frog. 'You'll set out into the world to seek your fortune, and Puppy and Kitten and I will come with you. And I have a friend who I know would like to come too, and that is a pony. His master has gone abroad and left him, and he is feeling very lost and lonely. You shall play on your pan pipe, and Puppy and Kitten and Pony and I will dance. A crowd will gather in every village to watch the performance, and when it's over one of us will go round with your old cap. If the people don't drop their pennies into it – my name isn't Frog. Now cheer up and play up; I'll call Pony and we'll have a rehearsal.'

'Oh yes, yes, what fun!' cried Puppy and Kitten. 'Let's have a rehearsal!'

So off went Froggie and soon came back followed by a little chestnut pony.

'Good morning, Pony,' said Jack. 'would you like to join us on our travels?'

'Oh yes, yes please!' said Pony. 'I don't like being left alone.'

So Jack began to play on his pan pipe, and Froggie and Kitten and Puppy and Pony began to dance. Kitten sprang, Puppy leaped, Pony danced as if he had springs in his hoofs, and as for Froggie, one moment he was standing on his head, and the next moment he was turning somersaults, and the next he had his feet in his hands and was twirling round and round, fast enough to make a body giddy. As Froggie danced he sang:

> *'Traff, traff, tra-ra-rip,*
> *See us hop, see us skip!*

Traff, traff, tra-ra-rance,
See us whirl, see us dance!
Traff, traff, tra-ra-ring,
Hear us laugh, hear us sing!
Traff, traff, tra-ra-rap!
Please throw pennies in the cap!

And by and by when Jack stopped playing, they all fell a laughing.

'Now,' said Froggie, 'up we get and on we go. *Forward marr-rrch!*'

They walked all day, because of course they had to get away from any place where Jack was known, before they gave their first performance.

When twilight fell they were all tired and all rather hungry, because they had only Jack's sandwiches to share between them, together with a lump of cake that he bought with his three pennies.

'Never mind, never mind,' said the cheerful Froggie. 'Tomorrow is another day, and with tomorrow comes our fortune.'

So they all cuddled up close together under a haystack and fell asleep.

And did their fortune come with the morrow? Yes it did. Their very first performance, which they gave on a village green, was a triumph. The villagers cheered and cheered; and when at the end of the performance, Puppy went round with Jack's cap, the pennies dropped into the cap thicker than hail falling. Now they never went hungry, and their living cost them very little, because they were sure to meet some friendy farmer or innkeeper, who allowed them to sleep at night in his barn or stable. Pony carried a big bag to hold their money, and by autumn that bag was bursting full.

But one early morning in late September, when they had been asleep in a big barn, Jack was awakened by some queer sounds. And starting up in surprise, he saw Froggie hunched in a corner, sobbing as if his heart would break.

'Oh Froggie, what *is* the matter?' cried Jack. 'Are you ill, have you got a bad pain?'

'No, I'm not ill,' whimpered Froggie, 'and I haven't got a pain, but I dreamed that I was back at the pool where I was born, and my mother was sitting on the edge of the pool wailing and shedding bitter tears. "Oh my

118

little son, my little son," she was crying, "Where are you? Are you still alive, or have the bad boys killed you?" And oh Jack, I can't bear to think of her being so unhappy!'

'And do you think my mother feels like that about me?' said Jack.

'Of course she does, of course she must,' sobbed Froggie.

'Then we must go home this very day!' cried Jack. 'Wake up, Kitten, wake up, Puppy, wake up, Pony, we're going home!'

Kitten and Puppy grumbled. They didn't want to go to Jack's house, they remembered how angry Jack's father had been when they were there before. And Pony was worried too. But Jack laughed, and said, 'When I show my Dad this bursting money bag, he'll be pleased enough to see you, I can tell you!'

So then and there they all set out on the road back to Jack's home. And Froggie was in such a hurry to reach the pool in the wood that he wouldn't let them stop to give a single performance on the way. 'If I find my darling mother has died of grief before we reach the pool, I shall never, never forgive myself,' he said.

But his mother hadn't died of grief. When the travellers reached the pool, they found her, just as Froggie had dreamed, sitting on a stone with her head bowed, and her queer little face covered with her queer little hands, and the tears dripping out between her fingers.

But when Froggie said, 'Darling mother, don't cry. Here I am!' Oh then how joyously she sprang up, and how she flung her arms round his neck, and how she hugged and kissed him, and how she listened all goggle-eyed to the tale of Froggie's adventures!

So Jack and Puppy and Kitten and Pony left Froggie there at the pool, and went on to the farm which was Jack's home. And there there was another scene of hugging and kissing, because Jack's mother had been just as unhappy about Jack as Froggie's mother had been about Froggie.

And as to Jack's father? Well, it was just as Jack had said. When he saw that bursting money-bag he was so delighted that he couldn't say one angry word. And when, after a hearty meal, Jack played on his pan pipe, and Puppy and Kitten and Pony gave an exhibition of their dancing — then Jack's father laughed and laughed.

'That's truly rare!' he said. 'That's something you don't see every day. We must give a party, and have all the neighbours in to see that!'

So now there was no question of driving Puppy and Kitten and Pony away. They lived happily with Jack and his parents ever after.

16. Wits But No Money

There was once a young man called Vanka who had plenty of wit, but scarcely any money. And Vanka often said, 'What a pity it is that I have so much in my head, and so little in my pocket!'

And one day a shopkeeper who heard Vanka say this said to him, 'Do you know what, Vanka, I will give you my money and I'll be your partner, because I should like to see what you can do with my money and your wits.' Then the shopkeeper gave Vanka all the money that he had put by.

And what did Vanka do with that money? He bought a great quantity of reed mats, and he sought now for a ship that would take them to Egypt. When he had found a ship and had agreed with the captain over the freight charges to Egypt, the captain asked him, 'And what is your cargo?'

'It is reed mats,' said Vanka.

The captain began to laugh. 'Listen, friend,' he said, 'it's no use taking mats to Egypt. Mats are much cheaper to buy in Egypt than they are here!'

Vanka answered, 'What does that matter to you, as long as you get your freight money?'

So the captain had all Vanka's reed mats loaded on to his ship; and they set sail for Egypt, in company with several other trading ships, full of various merchandise.

When the ships reached Egypt, the other merchants began to unload their wares on to the wharfs and quays. But Vanka had all *his* reed mats carried to a great sandy beach, and laid out in a long row on the edge of the sea. Then he set fire to the mats and burned them to ashes. He sat down near the ashes and waited. In the night the sea horses came out of the water and licked up the ashes. In return the sea horses spat out precious jewels, diamonds, sapphires, pearls, rubies, emeralds and amethysts, all of an enormous size.

At daybreak next morning Vanka walked along the beach and picked up hundreds and thousands of jewels of inestimable value. He put these jewels in sacks, and packed them into his ship. When he had got all the sacks full of jewels into his ship, he put a load of bricks on top of the sacks.

The other merchants, having loading up their ships with various valuable merchandise, were ready to return home. When they saw Vanka's cargo of bricks they just laughed. 'Haven't we enough bricks at home?' they asked.

'I thought we could do with a few more,' said Vanka.

The merchants looked at one another and shook their heads. 'The poor lad has surely lost what little wits he ever had,' they said.

Well, they all sailed off homewards. When they landed at their home port, they must, by custom, take a sample of their merchandise as a present to the Emperor. All the merchants went up to the Emperor's palace to present their gifts, and Vanka with them. Vanka was carrying something wrapped in a cloth. 'You can't take *bricks* to the *Emperor!*' laughed the merchants. But Vanka didn't answer them.

So they came into the Emperor's presence and presented their gifts.

Vanka stood silent, and the Emperor said to him, 'And you, brick merchant, what gift have *you* brought me? Vanka gave the Emperor the something wrapped up in the cloth. The Emperor unwrapped it. What did he see? Two huge rubies of priceless value, the like of which he had never seen before in all his life.

For a moment the Emperor was speechless with delight and astonishment. Then he asked, 'And have you more stones like these?'

'Oh yes,' said Vanka. 'If your majesty will be pleased to accept such stones, I have a whole ship full of them.'

Well, of course his majesty *was* pleased to accept such stones! In return he gave Vanka a handsome sum of gold and a dukedom.

Vanka did not forget the shopkeeper, who had given him the money to buy the reed mats, and to hire the ship that took him to Egypt. And with the shopkeeper Vanka now shared all his good fortune.